MESSAGE FROM VENUS

The wineglass spelled out V-E-N; but then it
faltered, as if uncertain where to go next. I held my
breath, half scared, half hopeful. Suddenly it
skidded across the table to the U and the S.

GONE TO VENUS.

'Aaah!' Ma let out her breath in a long,
triumphant sigh. 'I should have known.'

'Known what?' I demanded. 'Venus isn't a place,
it's a planet.'

She made no comment.

I glanced uneasily at Aisling. Her eyes were wide
open, as if the message had taken her by surprise.

'Ma,' I said, very gently, 'you're surely not
suggesting that Dad's gone to another planet?'

Tessa Krailing was born in Kent and brought up in Sussex. She wrote her first story when she was four. From that moment, she knew that she wanted to be a writer, but it took her a long time to realize her ambition. First she worked as a television drama production secretary for the BBC, then decided to switch careers and trained as a teacher. Writing took a back seat until she happened to write a story for the dinosaur-mad children in her class. *A Dinosaur Called Minerva* became her first published book and she enjoyed writing it so much that she decided to give up teaching and concentrate on writing full time, initially for a trial year. That was fifteen years ago. Since then she has written many books for children of all ages. A revised and updated version of her book for adults, *How To Write for Children*, which originally appeared in 1988, will shortly be published.

Tessa Krailing now lives on the Isle of Wight where she occupies her time reading, writing and walking along the beach in search of inspiration.

'Krailing's grip on her craft is sure.'
The Guardian

To Joyce Windsor, with love

TESSA KRAILING

MESSAGE FROM VENUS

RED FOX

A Red Fox Book

Published by Random House Children's Books
20 Vauxhall Bridge Road, London SW1V 2SA

A division of Random House UK Ltd
London Melbourne Sydney Auckland
Johannesburg and agencies throughout the world

1 3 5 7 9 10 8 6 4 2

First published in Great Britain by
Hutchinson Children's Books 1996

Red Fox edition 1997

Printed and bound in Great Britain by
Cox & Wyman Ltd, Reading, Berkshire

Papers used by Random House UK Limited
are natural, recyclable products made from wood grown in
sustainable forests. The manufacturing processes conform to
the environmental regulations of the country of origin.

RANDOM HOUSE UK Limited Reg. No. 954009

ISBN 0 09 965661 2

1

'Now close your eyes,' Ma said, 'and let your minds go blank.'

My mind was already blank. It couldn't have been much blanker. We – that is my mother, my older sister Aisling and me – sat round the kitchen table with the Lexicon cards arranged in a circle and our fingertips resting on an upturned wineglass. We were not playing games. Quite seriously, we were trying to find out where my father had gone.

'It's moving,' Aisling said.

She was right. I felt the glass slide away beneath my fingers and opened my eyes to watch. One of us must be pushing it, either consciously or unconsciously, and I felt pretty sure it wasn't me. I glanced suspiciously at Ma. She was concentrating so hard that a sheen of sweat had appeared on her broad, pale brow. Was it her wishful thinking that sent the glass travelling across the table towards the G, then O and N and E?

GONE.

'Oh, brilliant!' I muttered with heavy sarcasm. 'I mean, it's not exactly telling us anything we didn't already know, is it?'

It was now two months since the night Dad went for a walk on the Common to observe the stars and never returned. The police had searched for him and so had the Sally Army, without success. My own theory was that he must have lost his memory. He had always been forgetful about birthdays and things like that, so it seemed quite possible that he could have wandered off somewhere and absentmindedly started a new life. I found the idea comforting, because there was always the hope that one day he'd get his memory back and come home.

But Ma was too impatient to sit around waiting. First she had searched every bush and hollow of the Common herself in case the police had missed a vital clue. Then she visited the hostels and soup kitchens and the damp, dark places where the homeless hang out. Finally, out of sheer desperation, she had started to use less orthodox methods, such as taking Dad's hairbrush along to a medium who claimed to divine where a person was by holding something they'd used every day. But that hadn't worked either, and now she had resorted to the wineglass, which seemed to me a crude and unreliable method by anyone's standards, let alone a person as sensible and down-to-earth as Ma.

Hello, it was off again. This time it headed for T and then O.

'Gone to –' Aisling announced. She wore a faraway look, her eyes hidden by heavy white lids with a fringe of ginger lashes. As usual, I couldn't make out what she was thinking. She was four years older than I was – nearly seventeen – but the gap was more than just age. She was a risk-taker, like Dad; desperate to leave school early and become an actress. Whereas I was a naturally cautious plodder, like Ma.

The wineglass spelled out V-E-N; but then it faltered, as if uncertain where to go next. I held my breath, half scared, half hopeful. Suddenly it skidded across the table to the U and the S.

GONE TO VENUS.

'Aaah!' Ma let out her breath in a long, triumphant sigh. 'I should have known.'

'Known what?' I demanded. 'Venus isn't a place, it's a planet.'

She made no comment. It was hard to tell what she was thinking because since Dad disappeared her round face had worn a closed look, as if she had shut herself inside the castle of her innermost thoughts and pulled up the drawbridge.

I glanced uneasily at Aisling. Her eyes were wide open, as if the message had taken her by surprise. This seemed to confirm that it wasn't her pushing the wineglass around.

'Ma,' I said, very gently, 'you're surely not suggest-ing that Dad's gone to another planet?'

'It's not me suggesting it,' she said. 'It's the wineglass. Shall we go on?'

3

I didn't want to go on; but there was something compulsive about the whole set-up – the candle-light, the darkness outside the window, our three faces staring down at the cards. Beneath my fingers the wineglass seemed to tingle. Furtively I eased them off, just a fraction. 'Okay. What shall we ask it next?'

'Let's try to find out what happened,' said Ma. 'That night on the Common, I mean. If he met someone.' She noticed I was no longer touching the glass. 'Come on, Rose.'

Reluctantly I replaced my fingers. The idea that we might be directly communicating with Dad gave me the shivers. Surely this method was only supposed to work if you wanted to contact the dead? So if we were really getting through to Dad . . . Oh, I hated this morbid game!

The wineglass spelled out MEN.

'He met some men,' Ma stated. 'From Venus? But why did they come here?'

The answer we got was MESS.

'It keeps going to the same letters,' I pointed out. 'Anyway, MESS must be wrong. It doesn't make sense.'

'It does if you remember what your father believed,' said Ma. 'He always said we've made such a mess of life on earth that we'll never be able to put it right without help from outside.'

'You mean a mission from another planet?'

'Perhaps,' she said, still not looking me in the eye.

4

I couldn't believe we were having this conversation. Aisling, I noticed, was keeping quiet. It was up to me to sound a note of sweet reason. I said, as tactfully as possible, 'But Ma, if they were friendly why should they kidnap Dad?'

'I don't know.' She closed her eyes again. 'Why did they take you away with them, Dermot?'

The wineglass spelled out TRAIN.

I gave a snort of laughter, partly from nerves. 'That proves it's rubbish. He couldn't possibly have gone to Venus by *train*!'

Ma looked thoughtful. 'Not *by* train,' she said. '*To* train. Maybe they're teaching him how to save us from extinction. Then they'll send him back as their agent.'

She spoke with such conviction that I could almost believe her, but of course the wineglass was only saying what she wanted it to say. It could have spelled out any old rubbish and she'd have made it fit somehow.

She added, 'Let's ask how soon—'

I pushed back my chair. 'Sorry, Ma, but this is getting too spooky for me. I'm going to bed.'

She looked disappointed, but only said, 'Don't forget to clean your teeth.'

I was reassured by this last remark. It showed that basically she was still the same old practical Ma.

'And don't use all the hot water,' Aisling called as I closed the door behind me.

* * *

Upstairs in my room I brushed my hair and thought about Venus. Okay, so it was true Dad had been obsessed with that bright, mysterious planet. Recently, just before he disappeared, he had started writing a book about it. But Ma coming out with all this stuff about him being taken off to live there... Frankly, it made me nervous.

The irony was that Ma had never had any patience with Dad's stargazing. She was furious when he spent hundreds of pounds on an astronomical telescope and set it up in the attic. There's enough trouble here on earth, she used to say, without worrying about outer space. In fact astronomy was a fairly recent hobby for him. He'd only taken it up when we moved into this house two years ago, after my grandmother died and left it to my mother in her will.

Coming to 4 Oakfield Avenue had been a culture shock for all of us. Up till then we had lived in rented flats, and were in the habit of moving on average about once every eighteen months. Dad liked impermanence: being stuck in one place made him jumpy. He had wanted to sell the house straight away and invest the money, but Ma dug her toes in. This was her home, she said, and anyway she was sick of rented flats. After a monumental row Dad gave in, but he had never really liked living in the large, semi-detached, respectable Edwardian villa. He said it made him feel middle-aged.

'But Dermot, we *are* middle-aged,' Ma reminded

him. They had married quite late in life and Ma was thirty-six when Aisling was born. Now they'd both turned fifty, but Dad said he didn't feel it. He didn't think he'd ever feel fifty. Inside he would remain twenty-four for ever.

About an hour later I heard Aisling's footsteps on the landing. I waited until she'd gone into her room, then put on my dressing gown and crept along to knock on her door. 'Aisling, it's me. Can I come in?'

'It's late.'

'Yes, I know.' I opened the door and peered in. 'But I need to talk.'

'Okay.'

I was surprised how quickly she gave in. Maybe she too needed to talk.

She sat at her dressing table, wiping off her lipstick. It was all the make-up she used. Her skin was matt white with freckles, typical colouring for a redhead. She had a mass of hair and very small features, including a neat nose of which I was deeply envious. Mine had a bump in the middle, like Ma's.

I perched on the end of her bed. 'Sorry I chickened out, but I absolutely hate that sort of thing. Frankly, it scares me to death. Don't you think we should send for the doctor?'

'What for? Ma's not ill.' She tossed the used-up tissue on to the floor. Like Dad, she was happiest living in a tip.

'She must be, or she wouldn't have these wild delusions.'

Aisling sighed. 'Rose, if you send for the doctor he'll think it's you that's having wild delusions. He'll never believe it of Ma.'

There was truth in what she said. Ma, especially when she was in uniform – she worked as an auxiliary nurse at the local hospital – had an air of total sanity.

'Anyway,' Aisling went on, 'there's nothing wrong with her that time won't cure. It's just that she's finding it hard to accept that Dad's walked out on her. Of course she needs our help, but that doesn't mean calling in the doctor. What we have to do is play along with her till she gets over this crisis.'

She sounded so confident that I had to believe her. 'Where do *you* think Dad is?' I asked. 'Seriously, I mean.'

She stopped buffing her nails to stare into space. 'I don't know. But I can understand how he felt in this house. Trapped. Stifled. He had to escape or he'd have gone out of his mind.'

'You don't hate him for leaving us?'

She shook her head and started on her nails again. 'Wherever he is, I hope he's happy.'

'What happened after I left? Did the wineglass say anything more?'

'Yes, it said we're to start a community of watchers, seekers after truth like Dad, who believe there may be intelligent life on other planets.'

'You're joking!'

'I'm not joking. It spelt it out, every word.'

I stared at her, aghast. 'Where do we start this community?'

'Here, of course. We can't afford to move.'

'But how many – er, watchers are there going to be? We only have three bedrooms.'

'There's the attic. Ma wants you and me to bunk up there together. Then if she takes over your room that leaves two decent-sized rooms vacant, hers and mine. Three beds in each. Six people.'

'*Six*? Where's she going find them, anyway?'

She said, 'Dad will send them to us when the time comes, or she might advertise.'

'Advertise!' I was appalled. 'That means there'll be a lot of weirdos trooping in and out of our front door. Everyone in Oakfield Avenue will guess there's something peculiar going on, especially the Lehmans. And if they get hold of it, soon the whole world will know!'

Ralph and Enid Lehman were our next-door neighbours, brother and sister, both old maids, whose favourite pastime was poking their long noses into other people's business. Only this morning I had come face-to-face with Enid putting out milk bottles in her quilted paisley housecoat. 'No news of your father, I suppose?' she had asked in a hushed voice; and I had mumbled something vague and fled down the path.

'Sometimes, Rose, you can be hideously conventional.' Aisling slid the polisher back into her manicure case and stood up. 'Now go away. I want some privacy.'

'If we share a room,' I pointed out, 'you won't have any privacy. None of us will.'

She pushed me off the bed. 'Out.'

'And there'll be queues for the bathroom . . .'

'OUT!' She shoved me through the door and slammed it behind me.

Soon after I returned to my room I heard Ma come upstairs. She visited the loo, then went into her own room and closed the door. Would she let herself cry, I wondered, and did she sometimes feel lonely at night in the big old double bed? Not that Dad always slept in it with her. Sometimes he would spend all night in the attic with his telescope, or take it out on the Common to observe the stars, as he did two months ago.

I lay awake for hours. At school we had 'Preparation for Life' classes to teach us how to cope with sex and drugs and unemployment. But they didn't prepare you for anything like this.

So what's a person supposed to do when her father disappears and her mother decides he's gone to Venus?

2

Next day at lunchtime, when Matthew Barber and I took our sandwiches into the park, I told him about our wineglass session. He was the only one of my friends I could possibly tell without fear of being laughed at. Matthew was so serious he never laughed at anything, not even party political broadcasts; and he was obsessively interested in everything to do with our family, being potty about Aisling. Not that she gave him any encouragement. He was far too young. She considered him a wimp.

He listened gravely, looking rather like a Buddhist monk with his high, studious forehead and ruthlessly cropped brown hair. 'The problem is,' he said when I had finished, 'there's no corpse. If only your father had died—'

'Oh, thanks a million!'

'If only your father had died,' he repeated, 'your mother would be able to mourn. She'd wear black crepe and visit his grave with flowers. As it is, he's simply vanished into thin air, which leaves her with a lot of unanswered questions.'

'Such as?'

'Such as whether he's run off with another woman.'

This shocked me. It was true that Dad had loads of sex appeal for a man his age; and he'd also had plenty of opportunity to meet other women, being a carpet fitter. Well, he'd been a lot of things: carpet fitting was only his most recent job. But that he'd actually go so far as to cheat on Ma...

'No,' I said firmly. 'No, he'd never do that.'

'I'm not saying he did, only that it's one of the possibilities your mother has to consider. But naturally she doesn't want to face the fact that he may be shacked up with somebody else, so her unconscious has invented this story about him being taken to Venus. Psychologically, it's pretty run-of-the-mill.'

I had to take this seriously, because Matthew was good on psychology. His mother was a social worker.

'It gets worse,' I warned; and I told him about the community.

But he only said, 'That makes sense.'

'How can you say that? There's not an atom of sense in it as far as I can see.'

'On the contrary, it's the solution to all her financial problems,' Matthew explained patiently. 'Everyone knows that nurses don't get paid much, but she's luckier than most because she owns a house that she can turn into a source of income by taking in lodgers.'

'In that case why doesn't she come right out and say so? Why pretend it's because she's had a message from Dad?'

Matthew shook his head. 'It's no use expecting her to be rational. The only thing you can do is try to be supportive.'

Matthew was fond of words like 'supportive'. I reckoned he must have caught them from his mother.

I said gloomily, 'I wish there was somebody I could turn to.'

'You have me.'

'Yes, I know, but –' I tried to find a tactful way of putting it. 'I need to talk to an older person, somebody who's in a position to act.'

'You could talk to my mother.'

'No!' I spoke so sharply that he blinked. 'Promise me, Matthew, that you won't ever tell your mother. You mustn't tell anyone. I'll die if you do.'

He sighed. 'You worry too much about what people think, Rose. That's because you have low self-esteem.' After a pause he asked, 'What about your Aunt Eunice?'

He meant Ma's mother's sister – Aisling and I never bothered with the great-aunt bit – who was a seventy-two-year-old spinster living on the outskirts of town. I said, 'Aunt Eunice has trouble finding Channel 4. She'd never understand about Venus.'

'Don't you have any other relatives?'

I shook my head. 'Dad has some in Ireland, but we've never even met them. There's Uncle Pat in Liverpool, but he's not really an uncle, just an old friend of Dad's.'

'Give him a call,' Matthew said.

'Ma doesn't really approve of him. She thinks he was a bad influence on Dad. But I used to like him a lot.'

'Call him tonight, from a phone box. I'll come with you.'

'Okay.'

After school we had a hard job finding an un-vandalized public telephone. When at last we did I made Matthew wait outside. First I had to call directory enquiries to find out the number of the hostel for retired seamen where I knew Uncle Pat lived. Then, when I finally got through, some-one had to go off and fetch him, which took so long that I had time to read every bit of graf-fiti, thereby increasing my vocabulary by about 300%.

'Hello, hello, hello!'

'Uncle Pat? This is Rose.'

'Rose, Rose, by any other name...'

'Rose Kelly, Dermot's daughter. Don't you re-member me?'

'Dermot's daughter...' His voice changed, as if the line had suddenly cleared. 'Of course, I re-member you, Rosie. Saints, could I not remember

Dermot's own child, the very one I dandled on my knee as a babe!'

He was laying on the Oirish with a trowel, which I found a little off-putting. Outside the call box I could see Matthew hovering, his face white in the gathering dusk. Changing the receiver from my right hand to my left, I turned my back on him and muttered, 'Uncle Pat, I need your help.'

'Why, what's happened?' His voice sounded different, as if the line had suddenly cleared. 'Has Dermot returned?'

For a moment I was startled that he knew Dad was missing; but then I realised the police must have contacted him when making their enquiries. 'No, I wish he had. But – oh, I can't possibly explain over the phone. You couldn't come to see us, could you?'

'You want me to come to Braddon?'

'Yes, please. If you can spare the time.'

He said gently, 'You'd better tell me, Rosie – and don't be afraid I'll be shocked because there isn't much in this funny old world can shock Patrick Nolan. Are you in some kind of trouble?'

'It's not me,' I said. 'It's Ma.'

'Your Ma's in trouble?' He sounded incredulous.

'Well, not exactly. It's just that she's been acting rather strangely . . .' And because I badly needed to confide in someone, I told him everything.

When I'd finished there was silence. Then he said, 'Taking in lodgers, is it?'

'She doesn't call them lodgers. They're supposed

to be watchers. You know, people who believe in UFOs and things like that.'

'In that case I daresay she won't be charging much rent?'

I said doubtfully, 'She hasn't mentioned rent, but I expect they'll have to contribute something, if they're to be part of the community.'

'Community,' Uncle Pat repeated in a thoughtful tone. 'Now there's a word with a nice, cosy ring to it.'

'I don't know about cosy. That kind of set-up could attract all sorts of weirdos. I'm afraid she'll be taken advantage of. Someone's got to talk to her, persuade her to change her mind.'

'And what makes you think she'll listen to me? Her opinion of me was never high, you know. She's not likely to take much heed of anything I say.'

I said despairingly, 'There's no one else.'

There was a pause. Then he said, 'As it happens I do have some time on my hands just now. Yes, a trip down south might make a nice change. How about tomorrow?'

'That'd be great! But you mustn't let Ma know I rang you, or Aisling. If you tell me which train you're catching I'll meet you at the station. Then I can brief you before you arrive.'

I was pleased with that word 'brief'. It sounded sort of official.

'I don't like tying myself down to a special time. Best if I drop in casually, early evening maybe?'

'Oh, all right.' Suddenly I had misgivings. 'Uncle

Pat, you will be careful what you say, won't you? My friend Matthew always says it's dangerous to destroy someone's illusions unless you can replace them with something better.'

'Leave it to me, Rose darlin'. I'll be the soul of discretion, believe me.' The phone clicked.

I replaced the receiver slowly. I wanted to believe him. I wanted him to be an ally, someone I could confide in and trust, but I had a horrible suspicion he might turn out to be as unreliable as Ma had always said he was.

'Any luck?' Matthew asked when I stepped out of the call box.

'He's coming tomorrow.'

'Oh, good.'

He didn't sound too enthusiastic. I wondered if he was still miffed because I'd said I needed someone older.

'You can come to supper, if you like,' I said. 'Then you can meet him.'

'Okay. Thanks.'

We walked back across the park. Suddenly Matthew stopped dead and said, 'There it is.'

'There's what?'

'Venus.'

I followed his pointing finger. The sky was full of stars, pinpoints of light in a dome of dark blue velvet. They all looked much the same to me. I had never taken much interest in Dad's astronomy, at least not the way Aisling did.

'The bright one,' said Matthew. 'Just above the tennis courts.'

I stared at it hard, until my eyes began to water.

Matthew looked at me with concern. 'Rose, are you crying?'

'No,' I snapped sarcastically. 'I'm sending it a message. "Come home, Dad, all is forgiven." But I don't suppose he'll take any notice.'

Matthew took my arm as if I were disabled in some way. 'No,' he said sadly. 'No, I don't suppose he will.'

The following evening I went into the kitchen, followed by Matthew, to find Aisling taking a large batch of Cornish pasties out of the oven. 'Why so many?' I asked. 'Are we expecting visitors?'

Aisling shrugged. 'There's been another message.'

I groaned. 'Not the wineglass again!'

'She insisted on getting it out as soon as I got home.' Aisling's tone was flat, totally without expression.

'What did it say?' Matthew asked curiously.

Aisling shot him a hostile look. 'I wish you'd send your lover home, Rose. He gets on my nerves.'

'He's not my lover,' I said. 'He's yours.'

Aisling snorted. 'He should be so lucky!'

Matthew gazed at her with sickly adoration. 'I've been invited for supper.'

'In that case I'm off.' She untied the apron from her waist and hung it on the hook behind the door.

'Where?' I demanded.

'*My* business, beanpole.' The door slammed behind her.

Aisling liked to keep her private life private. In the evenings she mostly hung out in a theatre club frequented by other would-be actors. I knew this for a fact because one night Matthew and I had followed her there.

'You know what I reckon?' I said. 'I reckon she's ashamed.'

'Why should she be ashamed?' Matthew asked.

'She knows things are getting pretty weird, even though she tries to pretend it's normal. That's why she's stopped bringing her friends home, in case they laugh at us.'

Matthew looked unconvinced. 'Aisling's more complicated than you are,' he said. 'You're a very simple person, Rose.'

I knew he didn't mean it as an insult but somehow it sounded like one. I said curtly, 'Anyway, I'm glad she won't be here when Uncle Pat comes. She'd be furious if she knew I'd telephoned him. But why do you think she's made all these pasties?'

His eyes gleamed with anticipation. 'It'll be interesting to see how this develops.'

Sometimes I suspected that Matthew's interest in our family was largely clinical.

As for Uncle Pat, my feelings about him were confused, to say the least, and became even more so as the evening wore on and he didn't appear. We finished supper and went into the living room to watch a TV documentary about fruit bats. Aisling was still out and Ma seemed preoccupied. When the doorbell rang she said, 'Ah!' as if she had been expecting it. 'See who that is, Matthew, will you?'

I was glad she asked Matthew to go. It meant I had time to arrange a surprised/pleased/slightly puzzled expression on my face before Uncle Pat walked in.

He was shorter than I remembered and round as a barrel, with thin sandy hair and hazy blue eyes. Not a patch on Dad for looks, but with the same kind of laid-back charm. He advanced on Ma, holding out his hand. 'Hello, Francesca.'

She shook it limply. Her jaw had dropped several centimetres. Whoever she had been expecting it certainly wasn't Uncle Pat.

He swung round to look at me. 'Can this be Aisling? It's so long since we –'

'I'm Rose,' I interrupted, trying to warn him with my eyes not to overdo it.

'Of course it is! Rose, the dark one, like her mother.' He gave me a wink. 'Aisling's a copper-knob, the image of Dermot, as I recall. No doubt she's out somewhere in pursuit of pleasure. And this is . . . ?'

I introduced Matthew as a friend of the family. Uncle Pat shook hands with him and turned back to Ma, apologising for calling so unexpectedly and at such a late hour. 'But the strangest thing happened,' he said. 'Last night I was walking by the docks beneath the stars when all of a sudden, for no reason

20

in particular, the thought popped into my head that I must go and visit Dermot's wife Francesca.' He beamed at her. Her jaw dropped another couple of centimetres.

Matthew gave me a sharp dig in the ribs. 'Brilliant!' he muttered in my ear.

I said quickly, 'I'll get you some coffee, Uncle Pat. Would you like a Cornish pasty with it?'

'A Cornish pasty would go down a treat.' His face was bland and innocent as a baby's.

Matthew followed me out to the kitchen. 'Brilliant!' he said again. 'Did you hatch it up between you?'

'Hatch what up?' I banged a mug down on the table.

'The plot. It's cast-iron. Your mother will have to take notice of him now.'

'I don't see why.'

'Because she thinks he's been sent by your father. You can't fool me, Rose. Who thought it up – you or him?'

'He did, all by himself.' Viciously I spooned coffee into the mug. 'Matthew, go back. I want a full report on everything he says.'

3

By the time I carried the tray into the living room Ma had pretty well recovered from the shock, although she still looked a bit traumatized.

'... the time has come for me to leave Liverpool,' Uncle Pat was saying, 'and I've a mind to come south for a change. I suppose you couldn't direct me to some lodgings, Fran, not too pricey? My needs are few. I can sleep anywhere and have a small appetite.' He bit into a Cornish pasty, showering pastry over the carpet.

Ma said stiffly, 'You can stay here, Patrick.'

He gave an exaggerated start. 'My dear Fran, you don't mean it?'

'Yes, I do.' She lifted her chin. 'We'll be glad to have you. The girls are moving up to the attic anyway. You can have Rose's room.'

He didn't look at me. I don't think he dared. 'I can hardly believe my luck,' he said humbly. 'It seems like – like a gift from the heavens.'

Ma got swiftly to her feet. 'I'll make up the bed,'

she said. 'Rose can sleep on the folding bed in Aisling's room tonight.'

When she had left the room I said, 'Uncle Pat, how could you!'

He lifted his sandy eyebrows. 'How could I what, Rosie?'

'Trade on Ma's weakness like that. It's – it's not ethical.'

'I think it's brilliant,' Matthew said yet again.

Uncle Pat spread out his hands. 'What else could I do? You know your mother doesn't approve of me. She'd never listen to me in the ordinary way of things. But if she thinks I've been sent by your father ... well, I can't see the harm in it meself.'

'Neither can I,' said Matthew.

I said unhappily, 'It seems like cheating.'

'Listen, Rosie.' Uncle Pat drew me down beside him on the sofa. 'We have a delicate situation here and it's important we tread with care. Like you said, this community idea could attract all kinds of weirdos and your mother has to be protected. Isn't that so?'

'Well, yes...'

'I'm here to see that nobody takes advantage of her.' His eyes brimmed with sincerity. 'For Dermot's sake.'

'Okay,' I said weakly. 'But you'd better behave yourself, that's all.'

'Rose darlin', I'm an angel. Don't be fooled by my lack of wings.'

Some angel!

When Aisling came home she shook me awake. 'What the hell are you doing in my room?'

I struggled out of a dream tunnel full of fruit bats and Cornish pasties. 'You're very late...'

'Never mind about me. Why aren't you in your own bed?'

I giggled. 'There's a man in it.'

She shook me again. Her hair with the light behind it looked like a halo of copper fuse-wire. 'What man?'

'Uncle Pat.'

'*Who?*'

By now I was properly awake and on my guard. I propped myself on my elbows. 'Uncle Pat from Liverpool. He just dropped in by chance and Ma invited him to stay.'

Aisling straightened. 'I don't believe you. She loathes the man.'

'Not any more. She thinks Dad sent him. He's to be the first member of our community.'

She stared down at me. I could feel the cold coming off her, the cold from outside, like an icy aura.

'And tomorrow,' I added, rubbing it in, 'you and I have to move our beds up to the attic, to make room for the others. I expect they'll be arriving in droves any day now.'

She was silent.

'I don't suppose you thought it would happen,' I

went on. 'You didn't think there was the slightest danger anyone would actually turn up, did you? But you were wrong...'

'I'm going to the bathroom.' She grabbed cleansing milk and cotton wool from the dressing table. Halfway through the door she turned round and stuck her head back in. 'And don't think for one minute you've fooled me. I know you had a hand in this somewhere.'

Next morning there was only Ma and me at breakfast. I'd left Aisling still sleeping in the curious way she had, lying flat on her back like a corpse and breathing in little gentle sighs. So far there was no sign of Uncle Pat.

Ma seemed remarkably calm, considering. She even hummed to herself as she scrambled eggs for the two of us, and fried bacon for me. She always watched her weight. Not that it made any difference: she had been a size 16 ever since I was born and wouldn't look right any other way.

Eventually I could keep quiet no longer. 'Wasn't it strange,' I blurted out, 'Uncle Pat turning up like that, right out of the blue?'

'Very strange,' she agreed. 'Not that someone should turn up, of course, but that it should be Patrick Nolan of all people. Still, your father knows best.'

'You really think Dad sent him?'

She tightened her lips. 'Time will tell. But that's

the lesson we have to learn, to expect the un-expected.'

She sounded so sure that I almost believed her, even though I knew Uncle Pat to be an impostor. On the other hand, perhaps it was *meant* that he should come here. Perhaps, in asking him to come, I had been an instrument of fate?

Or of Venus . . .

I told myself not to be idiotic and reached for the orange juice.

'By the way,' Ma said, 'I've invited Aunt Eunice for lunch next Sunday. That means either you or Aisling will have to fetch her.'

'Not me.' Aisling came into the kitchen in her dressing gown, purple silk with a green dragon on the back. Her face was milky-pale, her hair a flaming tangle. 'I have to go out on Sunday morning.'

I said quickly, 'I have to go out too. I promised to meet Matthew.'

'Then you can take him with you to fetch Aunt Eunice,' Ma said. 'Matthew's good with old people. He doesn't bully them.'

'Aunt Eunice isn't old,' I grumbled. 'Seventy-two's nothing these days, you have to be over eighty to be old. Why can't she come on the bus by herself?'

Ma said reproachfully, 'You know she gets con-fused on buses. Last time she came on her own she ended up at the depot.'

'Okay, okay.' I glared at Aisling. '*Some* people never seem to pull their weight.'

But she only smirked and turned her head away.

Aunt Eunice was like a sparrow with permanently ruffled feathers. Her small brown eyes were constantly on the move and she had two pairs of spectacles – one for reading and one for distance – suspended on chains around her neck. When Matthew and I rang her doorbell she refused to let us in until she had peered at us through the spy-hole, after which it took several more minutes for her to undo all the bolts and locks that protected her one-bedroomed, first-floor flat from possible intruders.

'One can't be too careful nowadays,' she said when she finally let us in.

I noticed she was wearing carpet slippers and her old brown pully with holes at the elbows. 'Have you forgotten,' I asked, 'that Ma's invited you for lunch?'

'Of course not,' she said with dignity. 'Just a mo while I put some lipstick on.'

While we waited Matthew stroked the cat, Boris. It was a large, ill-tempered beast, frosty with females but inclined to be coy with the male sex, which Matthew said proves how neutering can give a cat hangups. It even let him tickle its overblown stomach, whereas if I dared to approach, it narrowed its yellow eyes and flexed lethal-looking claws.

Aunt Eunice reappeared, her mouth a bright red smudge. She wore an old musquash coat with a round, brimless hat in khaki felt. 'Ready,' she said brightly.

27

'I can't,' said Matthew, looking sick. 'I can't travel on a bus with someone wearing the skin of a dead animal.'

'In that case,' I said, anxious to get home so that I could keep an eye on Uncle Pat, 'you'll have to run along behind.'

He compromised by sitting two seats away from us and gazing resolutely out of the window. Neither of us noticed, till we got off the bus, that Aunt Eunice was still wearing her carpet slippers.

'Honestly, Rose,' Ma said when we arrived, 'you're as bad as she is. What if it's raining when it's time to take her home?'

With a shrug I said, 'Matthew can carry her piggy-back. Heaven knows she doesn't weigh much.'

Matthew looked even sicker, but when Aisling returned she was in such a good mood that she spoke quite kindly to him and even suggested he stayed to lunch. This stunned him into a kind of rapturous stupor.

'Where's Uncle Pat?' I asked.

'Still in bed,' Ma said. 'He's hardly got up since he arrived.'

Aunt Eunice, hunting in the sideboard for some sherry, looked up in alarm. 'You've a man in the house?'

I explained about Uncle Pat. She didn't remember him, of course, but wasn't at all reassured to learn he was a friend of Dad's. She had always regarded Dad with the utmost suspicion.

'Really, Francesca.' She turned her anxious, darting eyes on Ma. 'Is this wise?'

'I don't seem to have any choice in the matter,' Ma said enigmatically.

Aisling said, 'There may be more, Aunt Eunice. Ma's expecting them any day.'

'More men?' Aunt Eunice found the sherry bottle and clutched it to her non-existent bosom.

'Or women,' said Ma. 'It depends who turns up.'

Aunt Eunice, sensing there was something going on she didn't understand, tipped up the bottle till her glass overflowed.

We were about to take our places at table when Uncle Pat appeared, his shirt partly unbuttoned to reveal a grizzled hairy chest. He sniffed the air. 'Ah, roast lamb. Would you like me to carve, Francesca?'

Ma looked a bit taken aback. Nonetheless she invited him to sit at the head of the table, in the chair nobody had sat in since Dad disappeared. Aunt Eunice stared at his naked chest with uneasy fascination. Aisling smiled at her plate. Uncle Pat rolled up his sleeves and took up the carving knife.

Gradually I began to relax. He set himself out to charm, and charm he did, even Aunt Eunice, who was getting tipsier by the minute. When this was her sister's house, she said, they used to keep a very elegant table. Life was so pleasant in those days, none of the terrible things you hear about nowadays, everyone behaved themselves. She had always felt so safe in this house . . .

I caught Uncle Pat's eye and felt like a conspirator. I looked away again quickly and helped myself to more vegetables. Conspiracy seemed to be making me hungry.

After lunch Matthew helped Aisling and me carry our beds up to the attic, and by the time we went downstairs again Uncle Pat and Aunt Eunice were both snoozing in armchairs. We settled down to watch TV until eventually it began to get dark outside.

When the doorbell rang Ma looked up and said 'Ah,' just the way she had done last night. Matthew was playing chess with Aisling and didn't want to move, so it was me who opened the door. On the doorstep stood the most beautiful person I had ever seen in my life. He was tall with golden skin, brass-coloured hair and blue, bottomless eyes. I gaped at him, speechless.

'You must be Rose,' he said in a deep, melodious voice. 'I'm Gabriel and I think your mother's expecting me.'

4

It was freezing cold in the attic. Looking straight up through the skylight I could see about a dozen stars but none of them was Venus.

I said cautiously, 'Aisling, are you awake?'

She mumbled something I couldn't hear.

'What do you make of him?'

Mumble, mumble.

'He's fantastic-looking, don't you think?'

Mumble.

'But where's he come from? How did he know we were taking in lodgers? Who told him my name?'

No answer.

If only I hadn't had to take Aunt Eunice home. She was always twice as nervous after dark and babbled non-stop on the bus. Matthew again refused to sit with us and somebody laughed at her carpet slippers. I couldn't wait to get back and find out what was happening, but by then all the explanations were over and Gabriel already established in the room that used to be Aisling's. He hadn't brought any

31

luggage and had only the clothes he stood up in, holey jeans and a thin white T-shirt. Ma supplied him with a towel and a toothbrush – to be going on with, she said.

'It's a beautiful name, Gabriel.' I enjoyed rolling it around my tongue.

'Mmmm.'

'His hair's an amazing colour. Do you think it's natural?'

'No idea.'

'There's something strange about him, though. Are you sure he didn't say anything that might give us a clue? About where he came from, I mean.'

'Not a thing.'

The big question hung between us, but I dared not put it into words. Anyway, I couldn't believe he was an alien.

Or maybe I didn't want to believe it. There wasn't much point in falling for someone who might at any moment get himself dematerialized and teleported back to his own planet.

Suddenly I suffered a bad attack of sibling jealousy. I was well aware that Aisling was wildly attractive to look at. She took after Dad in that respect, whereas I was more your plain, homespun sort of person, like Ma. Matthew being goofy about her I could take, because my feelings towards him were strictly platonic. But Gabriel...

'Aisling.'

'What now?'

32

'I saw him first.'

'Don't be daft. You're only a baby, he wouldn't look at you twice.'

'That's not very kind!'

'It's the truth.' She yawned. 'Now belt up and let me sleep.'

For me, sleep proved impossible. The attic was full of memories of Dad. His books were stacked all over the floor – books that he had collected, mostly second-hand, about things like crop circles and ley lines and standing stones. Clearing a space for the beds, I had come across his own book, the one he'd been writing on A4 looseleaf notepads, and started reading the opening paragraph:

> **'If Earth is not the only life-bearing planet in the universe, which seems to me a reasonable assumption, then surely it's logical to conclude that other forms of intelligence must be watching us with great interest at this time. I say "at this time" because –** '

But at that point Aisling had interrupted by saying, 'Rose, move your bed under the skylight. I'm in a draught.' And I had done as she commanded because I knew from experience there wasn't any point in arguing with her. She always won. Anyway, I quite liked the idea of sleeping under the stars. Dad had put the skylight in specially, but soon afterwards he read a book by Patrick Moore saying it wasn't a good idea to observe from indoors, which was why he started taking the telescope on to the Common.

When I finally dropped off to sleep I dreamt that I was walking with Gabriel on some weird blue planet where the temperature was way below zero. In the morning I tackled Ma about putting some form of heating into the attic bedroom.

She said, 'You can take the electric radiator from the hall. That should make it warmer.'

'But Ma, it weighs a ton. I'll never manage it by myself.'

'Get Uncle Pat to help you.'

'Why not Gabriel? He's younger.'

'No harm in asking.'

I waited a beat before saying, 'Last night, when I answered the door, he said you were expecting him. Is that true?'

'In a way.'

'In what way?'

She turned away to stack last night's dishes in the sink, creating a clatter in which her reply – if she made one – was lost.

I followed her round the kitchen, determined to pin her down. 'Did Gabriel say he's been sent by Dad?'

'He didn't say he hadn't.'

'You asked him outright?'

She swung round, looking harassed. 'Rose, why are you cross-examining me? Can't you take anything on trust?'

'Well, you have to admit it's odd. I mean, he must

34

have got wind of the fact you were taking in lodgers.'

'Starting a community.'

'Whatever. He must have heard it from some-where.'

She poured tea into a mug. 'I hope you're not going to be hostile towards him. I'd like you to make him welcome.'

Somehow I seemed to have got myself on the wrong side of the fence. I said hastily, 'Oh, I'm not hostile, not in the least. I want to make him welcome.'

She looked relieved. 'In that case you can take him this mug of tea. I know he's awake because I heard him go to the bathroom.'

I carried the mug upstairs, reassured by this evidence of normality. It seemed unlikely that a genuine, bona fide messenger from Venus would need to go to the bathroom. I took a quick sideways look at my reflection in the landing mirror and felt reasonably pleased with what I saw. At least my hair, being straight, didn't get into a tangle overnight, like Aisling's.

When I knocked, his voice came back at once, inviting me to come in. I found him sitting up in bed and was immediately thrown into confusion by the sight of his bare brown chest above the bedclothes. But of course he'd had to sleep in the nude, he'd brought no luggage.

'Ma thought you'd like some tea.' I approached as near as I dared to the bed, holding out the mug at arm's length.

'That's kind of her.' His smile was dazzling. 'And how are you this morning?'

'Quite well, thanks.'

This wasn't the conversation I'd imagined, but I was still so knocked out by his physique that my brain seemed to have gone into reverse. Unfazed by my presence, he leaned back against the pillows. Truly he was beautiful, even first thing in the morning. I could see now that his hair had white-blond streaks in it and he wore a half-humorous, half-knowing look, as if he could read my thoughts. But he said nothing. It occurred to me that this was a sign of total self-confidence, to lie there without uttering a word.

Suddenly I realized I was standing on one leg, teetering like a nervous infant. This was not creating the impression I intended. Planting both feet firmly on the ground I said gruffly, 'Are you proposing to stay here, may I ask?'

'You may.' His voice was gentle, forgiving my lack of grace. 'Yes, Rose. Your mother has invited me to become a member of her community.'

'She's told you about it?'

'Of course.'

'Did she tell you the idea behind it? Has she – ?' I found this difficult to say. 'Has she mentioned my father?'

'Not yet.'

The way he said this implied she didn't have to tell him, he already knew. For some reason it made me angry, not at him exactly but at the shamefulness of our situation. I supposed I should be grateful he wasn't laughing, at least not openly.

I said defensively, 'It's quite a shock when a person's husband disappears. A shock like that can give a person strange ideas.'

'You think it's strange to want to save the earth from being destroyed?'

'Well, no. But –'

'Somebody has to do something about it soon, you know, or it'll be too late.'

'Oh, I agree. But expecting help from another planet...' My voice tailed off. I hadn't the courage to say what I really thought.

He set the mug aside and flung back the bedclothes. 'You'd better leave, Rose. I'm going to get dressed.'

I fled. It wasn't until I got outside that I remembered I'd meant to ask him to help me carry the radiator upstairs, but I dared not go back.

Instead I looked in on Uncle Pat. He was dead to the world and didn't even wake up when I bellowed in his ear. The room which used to be mine now smelt of stale whisky and sweat. It was only then that I realized Gabriel's room had smelt quite different, fragrant and fresh, like – like bath oil. *Our* bath oil.

Well, that wasn't so surprising. He must have taken a bath and helped himself. Fair enough, after such a long journey.

What long journey? *Steady, Rose,* I told myself sternly. *You're in danger of losing your grip on reality.*

* * *

My chief female friend at school was Victoria Ironside. The most interesting thing about Victoria was that although she was shorter than I was she had huge bosoms already, of which I was secretly envious. Not even Aisling had bosoms like that.

During Eng. Lit. I told her, rather rashly, that I was in love.

She propped up her copy of *The Woman in White* and behind it demanded, 'Who with?'

'His name's Gabriel.'

'Where did you meet him?'

I cast a wary eye at Mr Wesley, otherwise known as the Weasel, but he was sneakily marking another class's exercise books and not looking in our direction. 'He's come to be our lodger.'

'Your mother's taking in lodgers?'

'She has to, to make some money.'

'Poor thing.' There was more complacency than pity in Victoria's voice. Her father's Volvo was this year's model and her mother went to the hairdresser twice a week.

'Gabriel's the first, apart from Uncle Pat.' I felt the need to impress. 'He's the best-looking bloke you ever saw.'

'I'd love to meet him. Can I come home with you tonight?'

'Better not,' I said hastily. 'We're a bit busy just now.'

'You never ask me home these days.' She looked hurt. 'You ask Matthew.'

'Matthew's different. He's almost part of our family. What I mean is, we hardly notice he's around...' I was beginning to wriggle. It was a relief when the Weasel said, 'Rose Kelly, do I hear you talking?'

He always picked on me, never on Victoria. This may have had something to do with the fact that her father was his bank manager. I pleaded guilty, he reminded me there was an assessment coming up, and the lesson ended on a sober note.

After school Victoria insisted on accompanying me to the bus stop, but Matthew was already there and between us we managed to freeze her out. Luckily she lived in a different part of town – the posh part – so when the bus came we waved goodbye and left her staring after us. We spent the journey talking in low voices. Matthew was fairly noncommittal about Gabriel. He said he found him 'interesting'. I, with a smirk, said so did I.

We got off the bus to see Uncle Pat coming out of the betting shop on the other side of the road and hurried to catch him up.

'Uncle Pat,' I said reproachfully, 'you're being no help.'

He showed no sign of remorse. 'Give me time, Rose darlin'.'

'You've had plenty of time,' I pointed out, 'but you've spent most of it asleep.'

'Recouping my energy. I was worn out when I

arrived. It takes a while to get over a journey like that, you know.'

Travelling from Liverpool to Braddon hardly seemed an adequate excuse for jet lag. 'But when are you going to *do* something?' I asked.

He sighed. 'First I need to win your mother's confidence. She must learn to trust me enough to tell me what's on her mind.'

'He's right, Rose,' Matthew said. 'You can't rush things in a situation like this.'

'Softly, softly,' Uncle Pat agreed. 'Anyway, we should know more after tonight.'

'Why tonight?' I asked.

'Your mother's called a meeting after supper, the first meeting of the community. She says she has something important to tell us.'

5

'First,' Ma said, 'we have to sort out who's going to do what.'

We were seated around the kitchen table, Ma at the head with Gabriel on her right. Matthew had asked if he could stay and she said yes, he could be an associate member of the community, although of course he couldn't sleep here overnight, his mother might not like it. (The truth was she probably wouldn't even notice.)

Ma went on, 'Gabriel and I had a good long talk this morning and we now have a much clearer view of what's needed. Isn't that right?'

She looked at Gabriel, who nodded gravely. He was still wearing his holey jeans but Ma had given him a clean shirt, one of Dad's. It was a sort of aqua colour that matched his eyes.

'The idea is,' Ma continued, 'that everyone should contribute according to his or her special talent. Financially we need to be self-supporting, though not of course profit-making.' By now we were

41

hanging on her every word. She spoke with such authority, like a prophet. 'That's why I shall carry on working part-time at the hospital, so that I can pay the bills. Aisling will cook the meals.'

We all turned our heads to stare at Aisling. She looked down at the table and smiled. She had been smiling a lot these last two days, as if she had some secret pleasure.

Ma went on, 'She's been nagging me to let her leave school. Well, now I've given in. She's always enjoyed cooking. In fact you might call it her special talent.'

No wonder she'd been smiling! Aisling had always hated school. Not that she was stupid, but – like Dad – she wasn't good at living by rules and regulations.

'Patrick,' Ma went on, looking at him down the length of the table, 'will take care of the garden. The front can stay as it is, but the flowerbeds at the back will have to be dug up so we can grow vegetables instead, and maybe a little soft fruit.'

Uncle Pat looked unhappy. 'Well now, Francesca, that's a grand notion, to be sure, but the truth is I've been having a lot of trouble with me back lately. If it's all the same to you, I'd sooner take a job at the hospital. Portering or somesuch. If you were to put in a word on me behalf –'

Ma interrupted him. 'There aren't any jobs going at the hospital, and anyway portering's the last thing you should do with a bad back. So if you want to stay...?'

'I'll do the garden, Fran, if that's what you want.'
He added piously, 'For Dermot's sake.'

'Thank you, Patrick.'

I could keep quiet no longer. 'What about me, Ma?
What'll I be doing in the community?'

She looked at me soberly. 'We shan't be making
too many demands on you just yet, Rose. You've
enough to worry about, with your exams coming up.
The same goes for Matthew.'

Matthew accepted this. I felt less happy about it.
She hadn't mentioned my special talent, possibly
because she didn't think I had one.

'And Gabriel will guide our mental development.'
Ma brightened as she said this. 'He's already a lot
more advanced than most people, as I've been
hearing about today. In fact he says he's been
preparing himself for some time. As soon as he
heard about our plans for the community he knew
this was the chance he'd been waiting for.'

'How?' I asked. They all turned to stare at me.
'How did he hear about our plans?'

Ma looked at Gabriel. He said, 'I heard a voice,
Rose. Don't ask me where it came from, because
I've no idea. I only know that it told me to come
here.'

'Fancy.' Uncle Pat leaned forward, his blue eyes
guileless. 'You mean it actually gave you this
address?'

Gabriel smiled. 'Not in so many words, Patrick.
But the mind, when finely tuned, can act as a kind of

43

compass. It's simply a matter of following one's directional instincts.'

'You mean, like a homing device?' Matthew asked, with an air of scientific enquiry.

'Yes, Matthew, something of that nature. We're all high-frequency receivers, you know. The trouble is that most people don't bother to tune in.'

I was impressed, in spite of myself. 'Is that what you're going to teach us?' I asked. 'How to tune in?'

'I hope so, Rose.'

I liked the way he tacked our names on to everything he said. It made his words seem more personal. Fascinated, I asked, 'Is it anything like sound waves?'

'Very like, Rose.'

Matthew said, 'And you believe these sound waves come from Venus?'

We all held our breath. Ma broke the spell by saying, 'I don't suppose there's anyone here who doesn't know what Matthew is talking about, so perhaps now's the time for me to speak out?'

Gabriel said, 'Please do, Francesca.'

But at that moment, while everyone was waiting expectantly for the Great Revelation, the doorbell rang.

We let out a long, communal sigh. Ma said, 'See who that is, Rose, please.'

It was Aunt Eunice.

She stood on the doorstep surrounded by bulging suitcases and a wicker basket which mewed and shook with alarming violence. Behind her in the road a taxi drew away.

'They tried to break in,' she babbled, her small brown eyes darting wildly about. 'It was horrible, horrible!'

'Who tried to break in?'

'Youths. They rang my doorbell and shouted at me and pushed something nasty through the letter-box.'

I dared not ask what. She was hysterical enough already.

'I can't stay there. They might come back.' Her chin wobbled dangerously. 'I don't want to live alone any more. If Francesca's taking in lodgers I want to be one of them. After all, it was my sister's house once. I have a right to –'

Fearful the Lehmans might overhear, I yanked her inside and retrieved her luggage from the step. The wicker basket burst open and Boris sprang out, yellow eyes blazing and fur erect. With surprising agility for such a portly cat he leapt up on the tallboy and crouched there, spitting venom at me.

'He didn't want to come,' Aunt Eunice explained. 'But I told him it was for the best.'

I have to confess it, I enjoyed going back into the kitchen to announce, 'We've another member of the community. Somebody tried to break into Aunt Eunice's flat so now she wants to join us. And she's brought Boris with her.'

She appeared behind me. 'I've a right, Francesca. This used to be my sister's home. If she were still here she'd take me in. She wouldn't leave me at the mercy of muggers and rapists. I don't want to live alone any more. I want to be with other people...'

Ma got up from her chair and put her arms around Aunt Eunice's heaving shoulders. 'There, Aunt, don't cry. Of course you can join us. We'll be glad to have you.' Above Aunt Eunice's head she told us sternly, 'And that's another thing. We must be ready to open our doors to all sorts, however unlikely they may appear at first sight. The chances are they've been sent here for a purpose, even if we can't see what it is.'

We looked at Gabriel, as if for confirmation. His smile was slow in coming, but when it did it lit up the kitchen. 'Francesca's right. We must keep an open door.'

Aisling said tartly, 'All very fine, but where's she going to sleep?'

'In my room, for the moment.' Ma patted Aunt Eunice's back. 'It's lucky those new beds arrived this morning. Still, I suppose it's not to be wondered at. We're being guided, that's plain enough.'

Aunt Eunice lifted her head from Ma's chest. 'I'd prefer to have a room to myself, if you don't mind. I'm not use to sharing with other people.'

'Tomorrow, Aunt. Just for tonight you'll have to share with me. Aisling and Rose will make up a bed for you and Matthew can carry your luggage upstairs.'

When we passed through the hall Boris was still on

top of the tallboy and refused to be coaxed down, even by Matthew. But by the time we had made up the bed and come downstairs again he was in the living room, curled up smug-as-you-please on Gabriel's lap. On the chair opposite sat Aunt Eunice, her thin cheeks flushed, a cup of tea balanced precariously on her knees, telling Gabriel her life history.

'He's got them both eating out of his hand,' I said to Matthew when I went to see him off at the front door. He didn't want to go home, but Ma suggested it was about time or his mother would be agitating. In fact his mother never agitated if he was late, usually because she was even later herself.

'The guy has charisma,' Matthew said grudgingly. 'I'll give him that.'

'Loads of it,' I agreed. 'One can almost believe he does have mental powers, the way he seems to put people under a spell.'

'You're not suggesting he gets them from Venus?'

'Of course not. But you have to admit there's something special about him.'

Matthew looked at me in disgust. 'You just fancy him, that's your trouble.'

'Go home, Matthew!'

As he started down the path I turned to see Enid Lehman, in her quilted housecoat, putting out milk bottles again. It was incredible the way she timed it. 'Hello, Rose,' she said, her eyes bright as a squirrel's. 'You've got visitors, I see?'

'Yes, Aunt Eunice is staying with us for a few days. And Uncle Pat.'

'Would he be a relation of your father's?'

'No, just an old friend.'

'And the fair young man?'

'He's a – a cousin of ours. A distant cousin. Goodnight, Enid.' I closed the door firmly behind me and put the chain on, thinking how amazed she'd be if she knew how distant! But there I went again, half-believing that Gabriel had come from Venus, when of course I knew that was impossible.

Wasn't it?

6

I'd been feeling guilty about Victoria ever since
Matthew and I froze her out at the bus stop, so when
she asked me over to her house on the following
Saturday afternoon I said yes, even though I'd far
rather have stayed home with Gabriel.

Victoria was an only child, and she was spoilt
rotten. She had a room of her own decked out
in Laura Ashley fabrics where we sat playing tapes –
her taste in music was for treacly pop rather
than anything seriously decadent – while she showed
me the latest additions to her wardrobe. After
a while I got tired of saying, 'Oh, brilliant!' and
'Dead fantastic!' and started reading her teen
magazines instead; but then she accused me of
being a boring person and chucked the magazines
under the bed so that I couldn't read them any
more.

'Let's talk,' she said.

She talked, I listened. And all the time I was
thinking, *This is normal, this is how conventional*

double-parent families live. And I felt unbelievably superior.

Until she said, 'How's it going, your mother's boarding house?'

'It's not a boarding house. We – er, take in guests.'

'Guest-house, then. I don't know how you manage, with so little room. How many people have you got?'

'Two so far. Well, actually three, if you count Aunt Eunice.'

She looked aghast. 'But that means some of them are having to share!'

'Uncle Pat's moved in with Gabriel,' I said shortly. 'Aunt Eunice has my old room to herself and Aisling and I are sleeping in the attic.'

Her lip curled in distaste. 'God, how tacky.'

'Actually, I like it. I can watch the stars through the skylight when I'm lying in bed.'

She regarded me speculatively. 'I think we saw your Gabriel the other day. Mummy and I were driving past the end of your road – she'd just collected me from my piano lesson – and we saw this guy coming out of your gate. He was very tall and had dyed blond hair.'

'Could have been him,' I admitted, reluctantly. For some reason I felt annoyed that Victoria had seen him. She made everything sound so phoney and banal.

'Mummy said he looked quite presentable,' she added, which struck me as a typical Mrs Ironside remark. It was lucky they hadn't seen him wearing his holey jeans. Now Mum had given him a pair of Dad's chinos, which fitted him remarkably well. 'She asked me what he did for a living, but I couldn't tell her because you hadn't said.'

There was a question in her voice, which I ignored.

'So?' she prompted. 'What *does* he do for a living?'

'Nothing.'

'Nothing at all?'

'Not at the moment. He's – er, out of work.'

I hated saying that Gabriel was out of work. The Ironsides regarded anyone unemployed as a layabout.

'How did he get to hear you were taking in lodgers?' Victoria persisted. 'Is he a friend of Aisling's?'

'Of course not!'

'No need to bite my head off. He looks her type, that's all.'

'He's nothing like her type. She hardly takes any notice of him.'

'Well, I bet he takes notice of *her*, especially as they're living in the same house.'

'No, he doesn't. As a matter of fact he pays far more attention to me.'

Victoria stared at me. 'You're kidding!'

'It's true.' I made a show of looking at my watch. 'I must go.'

'Why? Mummy's expecting you to stay to dinner as you usually do.'

The Ironsides didn't have tea or supper. In the

51

evening they 'dined'. And it was always four courses, with soup or avocado for starters, and finishing with Stilton and grapes and genuine filter coffee. Usually I was happy to stay, because it appealed to the snob in me to sit at a polished table with dinner mats and silver candlesticks; but tonight I couldn't wait to get home.

'Sorry,' I said, 'but we're having a special evening, a sort of social get-together. I promised Ma I'd be back in good time.'

Victoria showed me to the door. Judging by her expression I had now undone all the good I'd hoped to do by coming here today. Travelling home on the bus I reflected sadly that if we were growing apart it was undoubtedly my fault. Victoria hadn't changed, I had.

And it was all due to Gabriel's mental development exercises.

'Ommm,' Gabriel intoned.

'Ommm, ommm, ommm,' we intoned back.

We sat in a circle on the floor of the front room with the furniture pushed aside. Most of us were cross-legged, except for Uncle Pat who was allowed to sit on a stool because of his bad back. Aunt Eunice managed amazingly well, even though her bones creaked and occasionally we caught a glimpse of pink lock-knit knickers. It was obvious she hadn't a clue what was going on, but if Gabriel had told her to take off all her clothes in Tesco's I believe she'd have done it. It was almost frightening, this power he had to make people do what he wanted.

In the centre of the circle burned a candle.

'Now be silent,' Gabriel commanded, 'and empty your minds.'

I wasn't much good at emptying my mind. It was far too cluttered. I tried to banish my guilty feelings about Victoria and to hold fast to a single thought, as Gabriel instructed, but it was no use. I was too aware of his face floating in the candlelight, and of Ma beside him in her navy-blue tracksuit with closed eyes and a frown of concentration. Matthew sat next to me, but I doubt if his mind was empty either, judging by the way he was staring at Aisling in her new green lycra catsuit. I was certain she had bought it with the intention of catching Gabriel's eye, no matter what she said. Although it didn't seem to be working because he hadn't looked at her once, at least not while I'd been watching, which was pretty well all the time.

'Try to slow down your breathing rate,' Gabriel ordered. 'We are entering a state of deep concentration.'

Uncle Pat shifted about on his stool with a pained expression. Aunt Eunice's eyes were tightly shut but her hands fidgeted with the spectacle chains hanging from her neck. The only one of us with a noticeably slowed-down breathing rate was Boris. He crouched on Gabriel's left, front paws folded, yellow eyes blinking in slow motion as if fighting off sleep. Only the occasional twitch of his tail betrayed his feline scepticism.

We had been doing these exercises for five days now. They were supposed to increase our control over mind and body and raise our level of consciousness. Gabriel's words, not mine.

His voice, quiet but emphatic, broke the silence. 'Lift up your hands. Stretch them high above you. Higher, higher. Now reach out and embrace the universe.'

Aunt Eunice turned scarlet with the strain, Uncle Pat looked likely to bust a gut. I fought down a terrible desire to laugh. Why was I playing along with all this?

Because I didn't want to upset Ma. And, to be honest, because I was afraid of offending Gabriel.

'Good. Well done.' His voice was quiet but emphatic. 'Now relax.'

Boris, as if on cue, rolled over on to his back, waiting for Gabriel to stroke his stomach. In five days he had become Gabriel's slave, deserting Aunt Eunice completely, but she didn't appear to mind. I had to admit she seemed happier since she'd come to live with us.

'It's over to you now, Francesca,' Gabriel said.

Ma eased her legs. I could tell she was suffering from cramp, but she wasn't going to admit it. 'Saturday night,' she began, 'will be different from the rest of the week. Our meetings will be longer, for a start, to give us time to discuss things.'

'What sort of things?' asked Uncle Pat.

She gave him a cool look. 'Important things, Patrick, about ourselves. Living together in a community means we have to help each other, but we can't do that until we know each other really well – and before we can do that we have to know ourselves.'

Gabriel nodded. 'Francesca's right.'

Ma went on, 'That means we have to be totally honest. We have to speak what's in our minds, not keep things bottled up inside.'

Gabriel nodded again. 'A problem shared is a problem solved.'

'So tonight,' Ma continued, 'just to start things off, we're each going to say what is our biggest problem.' She cast a slightly anxious look at Gabriel. 'Who should go first?'

'I think it should be you, Francesca.'

'All right.' She flushed slightly. 'Well, my problem is that I'm not very clever. Not intellectual, that is. I've never been able to read deep-thinking books or – or to answer the questions in those quiz programmes on the telly. Dermot was always the one with the brains. And – well, there were times when I felt I might be holding him back.'

Gabriel smiled at her. 'Thank you for being so honest, Francesca. Now the rest of you must be equally courageous. Eunice?'

Aunt Eunice jumped. 'I – I'm not sure. I haven't really thought. I mean ...' Her birdy brown eyes darted to Ma, then back to Gabriel. 'I suppose my problem is that I don't like living alone.'

'That problem is already solved, Eunice,' he said gently. 'You're part of the community now.'

'Yes, I am.' She looked suddenly radiant. 'In that case, I – I don't believe I have a problem any more.'

Gabriel smiled benignly at her. Then his face went blank. 'Aisling?'

'What?' Her tone was ungracious.

'Any problems?'

'None that I'm aware of.'

'That's very unusual. Are you sure you can't think of something?'

'Positive. Everything's going just swimmingly, thanks.' She opened her eyes wide, her expression as blank as his. 'Sorry.'

He sighed. 'In that case we'd better pass on. Rose, I hope you've given this more thought than your sister has?'

Put like that, what could I do? Giving myself no time to think I blurted out, 'I'm not a believer.'

He looked puzzled. 'A believer in what, Rose?'

'All this. Oh, I believe in developing our minds and all that, but not in the – well, you know.' I blushed, ashamed of my disloyalty to Ma. 'The Venus thing.'

'I see. Well, that's not a crime, Rose. There's nothing wrong with a little healthy scepticism. But don't close your mind to us entirely, that's all we ask. Matthew?'

'Er, I agree with Rose.' He added, by way of apology, 'I'm a scientist, you see.'

Gabriel said regretfully, 'In that case you do start with a certain disadvantage. Patrick?'

Uncle Pat shifted his weight and groaned. 'My biggest problem is me back.'

Ma said reprovingly, 'He means spiritual problems, Patrick.'

'It's hard to think about spiritual problems, Fran, when you're in agony. The rest of you should thank your lucky stars you don't have a problem like mine.'

Gabriel said, 'Bring your back to me, Patrick.'

Uncle Pat looked alarmed. 'You're not going to twist me spine around, are you? I went to one of those chiro-whatsits once and he damn near killed me.'

'I shan't even touch you. Bring it here.'

He shuffled over to stand in front of Gabriel. Gabriel made him turn round and then stared hard at his lower back. After a minute or so he asked, 'Can you feel anything?'

Uncle Pat frowned. 'Well, now you come to mention it, I believe I do feel something. A – a kind of heat.'

Gabriel looked pleased. 'Good. We'll repeat the treatment tomorrow. Don't expect miracles. It'll take time to cure you completely.'

I glanced round the room. Ma looked calm but happy, Aisling stared incredulously at Gabriel, Aunt Eunice's eyes brimmed with emotion. Matthew wore an expression of detached scientific interest.

Gabriel said, 'Let's take a break.'

7

'Auto-suggestion,' Matthew said.

He and I were in the kitchen, making coffee. The others had stayed in the front room, stretching their legs and talking in low voices.

'But Gabriel didn't even mention heat. So Uncle Pat must genuinely have felt something, he couldn't have made it up.'

'I'm not suggesting he made it up, only that he *imagined* he felt something.'

'He's not the imaginative type.'

'What other explanation is there?'

The kettle was belting out steam. I unplugged it, thinking that if I was absolutely honest I didn't even understand how electricity worked. Or television. Or computers. All of them were a mystery to me, yet I accepted them as part of my life, so why should I be surprised by anything Gabriel did?

As if he sensed my inward tussle, Matthew said sternly, 'Rose, I hope you're not wavering?'

'Of course not.' I poured boiling water over instant

58

coffee in the mugs. 'It's just that things are happening for which there doesn't seem to be any logical explanation. You must admit it's peculiar.'

'Oh, I do,' Matthew agreed. 'And do you know what I find most peculiar of all? Why Aisling doesn't go out in the evenings any more.'

I stopped loading mugs on to the tray and stared at him. 'Matthew, if your devious little mind is trying to work up some connection between her and Gabriel, forget it. They're not interested in each other.'

'That's *it*!' Matthew thumped the table with his fist. '*Why* aren't they interested?'

'Just because you're goofy about Aisling doesn't mean that every other guy has to be that way as well. She's not all that marvellous, believe me. You should see her first thing in the morning.'

Actually this was a libellous remark. Aisling looked sickeningly okay first thing in the morning. I lifted the tray. 'Coming?'

'There's something odd about it, that's all I'm saying.'

'*Matthew!*'

'Okay, okay.'

When we rejoined the others I looked hard at Aisling, who was sitting in the lotus position, breathing through her nose. Then I looked at Gabriel, who was talking quietly to Ma. He took a mug of coffee from the tray, at the same time giving me a slow, embracing smile. Basking in it, I convinced myself that Matthew was wrong, his obsession with Aisling had clouded his judgement, and if Gabriel was interested in anyone it was definitely me.

I gave Uncle Pat his coffee and squatted down beside him. 'How's your back?' I whispered. 'Is it any better?'

'Maybe,' he said cautiously. 'Maybe not.'

'But did you really feel the heat?'

He shrugged. 'I had to say something, didn't I?'

So he did make it up. I couldn't help feeling disappointed.

The coffee break over, Gabriel called us back into the circle. 'The time has come,' he said, 'for us to talk more about what Rose calls the "Venus thing". This may be a stumbling block for some. Nonetheless it's central to our life at the community, so I think Francesca should say a few words about what she knows.'

Ma looked tense. This was the first time she'd had to come right out in the open and say what she believed in front of other people. I wanted to shout, *Stop it! Can't you see she's sick? Why are you doing this to her?* But before I could utter a word Gabriel prompted her gently, 'Go on, Francesca.'

She drew a deep breath. 'I don't pretend to understand these things. As I've said before, I'm not a clever person and I don't have any scientific knowledge. I only know what Dermot's told me, and he says –'

'You've heard from Dermot?' Aunt Eunice looked alarmed. 'He's not coming home, is he?'

'No, Aunt,' Ma said wearily. 'He's not coming home. At least, not yet.'

'Once a drifter, always a drifter,' Aunt Eunice said with a sniff. 'You're better off without him, Francesca, take my word for it.'

Ma continued, 'It's no use asking me to explain what's happened because I can't. I only know what I know, that Dermot's alive and living in another place, which he calls Venus. Whether or not he means the planet I wouldn't like to–'

'There's no need to be so cautious, Francesca,' Gabriel interrupted. 'You believe he does mean the planet, don't you?'

'Well ... yes. Yes, I do.'

He smiled at her. 'Then have the courage of your convictions. Go on.'

'There's not much more to say. So far his messages have been mainly about the community. He's told me to expect people to arrive on my doorstep and – well, they have, haven't they?' Her tone was defiant.

Uncle Pat raised his hand. 'I'd like to ask a question, Fran, if I may be so bold? Do these messages still come to you through a wineglass?'

She stared at him. 'How did you know about the wineglass?'

'Rosie told me.'

'I see.' Her tone was cold enough to freeze the candle flame. 'Yes, it's true that at the beginning we had to use a wineglass, although it wasn't very satisfactory. For one thing, it was far too slow. Dermot was getting impatient.'

'He always was impatient,' said Aunt Eunice. 'He used to get very short-tempered with me at times.'

'But now we're moving into another phase. I believe this is why Gabriel has been sent to us, to help us communicate. These exercises we do, to improve our mental powers, are bound to make it easier for Dermot to tell us what he wants.'

'Thank you, Francesca,' said Gabriel. 'Now, if everyone's quite clear – ?'

'I'm not,' Matthew interrupted. 'I'd like to hear more about Venus.'

Gabriel looked pained. 'Very well, Matthew. Please put whatever questions you have to Francesca.'

Matthew turned to Ma. 'It's well known that Venus has an atmosphere even more hostile than Mars. Also, the clouds are made of sulphuric acid, not water vapour like here on earth, so how...?' His voice died away as he saw the expression on her face.

She said simply, 'It's no use, Matthew. I already told you, I can't answer those sorts of questions.'

His face turned dark red. 'Oh, well ... there's probably some quite simple explanation. I expect we'll find out eventually.'

I leapt to my feet. 'Okay, that's enough. Matthew, isn't it time you went home?'

They looked at me in surprise. But Gabriel said, 'Rose is right. We don't want to tax your powers of concentration too far in these early stages. Later, when the community's reached a higher stage of development, we shall be able to achieve more.'

Ma looked relieved. She stayed behind to talk to Gabriel, while I saw Matthew to the front door. Aunt Eunice said she would like to go to her room but couldn't remember where it was. As Aisling took her upstairs Uncle Pat came into the hall, muttering there was just time for a quick one before the pubs closed. He added quickly, seeing my face, 'Don't worry, Rosie, I shan't risk a hangover. This situation demands a clear head.'

Matthew said, 'I'll go with him, if you like, to make sure he keeps his word.'

'Thanks,' I said shortly. I had not yet forgiven him for pushing Ma so hard. He of all people should have realized how dangerous it was, but Matthew could be curiously dense at times. I suspected this was because he didn't really understand about feelings.

Ma and Gabriel were still talking in the front room when I went upstairs to bed.

Sharing a room with Aisling was a dead loss. She hogged the cupboard and wouldn't let me use her shampoo, and when we got to bed at night she didn't want to discuss things the way sisters were supposed to do but just lay there, flat on her back breathing so softly it was hard to tell if she was asleep or awake.

'Aisling,' I said tentatively.

'Mmmm?'

'Do you believe in Gabriel? I mean, do you think he's for real?'

No answer.

'He's very convincing,' I went on. 'All that stuff about training our minds and so on.'

She sighed. 'I wouldn't take it too seriously if I were you.'

'Why do you say that?'

'Because I wouldn't. Now go to sleep.'

Impossible. I kept remembering what Matthew had said about it being odd that she and Gabriel weren't interested in each other. In a way I agreed with him. They were both attractive people and it would have been only natural for them to be drawn together. Yet all the evidence was against it. Gabriel hardly took any notice of her and this evening she had been decidedly cool when he asked if she had any problems. And just now, when she told me not to take it too seriously, there had been a very sceptical note in her voice.

I said uneasily, 'Do you think we should talk to him? About Ma, I mean. I know you said we should play along with her, give her time to get over the Venus thing, but it seems to me this is only making her worse.'

No response. I lifted my head from the pillow to look at her. She had her eyes closed, but I could see the pupils working beneath her lids.

'Aisling?'

She turned her back on me, humping her shoulder. As I said, a dead loss.

8

Victoria said, 'And that's where I met him.'

My mind was on other things. 'Met who?'

'Rose, you haven't been listening to a word I've said!'

It was the morning break and we were standing by the drinks machine. The building was modern, all breeze blocks and wooden rafters, and the noise made by two hundred babbling schoolkids was deafening. Which was just as well, because Matthew kept following us around with a book he had found in the library about the planets.

'"...unbreathable carbon dioxide gas,"' he read aloud, '"and an atmospheric pressure ninety times that of the Earth. This acts like a blanket, building up temperatures at the surface to a furnace-like heat..."'

'What's he talking about?' asked Victoria.

'No idea.' I turned my back on Matthew and smiled at her encouragingly. 'Tell me about this boy you met.'

She was easily distracted. 'Oh, he's gorgeous. Dark velvety eyes and the most beautiful nose.'

He sounded like a spaniel. 'What's his name?'

'Shane. Isn't that romantic?'

Not so romantic as Gabriel. 'Do you think he'll ask you out?'

'He already has. We're going to a party next Saturday at Fiona Mackie's. Why don't you come with us?'

'She hasn't asked me.'

'That doesn't matter. She lives in a huge house, so one extra won't make any difference.' Victoria's eyes gleamed. 'Two extra. Bring Gabriel.'

'Oh, I don't think –'

'You said he was keen on you. I bet he'd jump at the chance.'

Matthew tapped me on the shoulder. 'It can come closer to the earth than any other planet and is similar in size. And it has craters, mountains and valleys, like Mars.'

'Matthew,' said Victoria. 'Get lost.'

He ignored her. 'What's especially interesting is that it spins in a clockwise direction – that's the opposite way to Earth and all the other planets. Now what do you make of that?'

'Not a lot,' I snapped.

All the same, it intrigued me. I started wondering whether it was in any way significant, if perhaps Gabriel was left-handed or did anything backwards. But then I remembered what Aisling had said last night, about him playing a game, and gave myself a mental shake.

'Oh, come on, Rose!' Victoria pleaded. 'You know I'm *aching* to meet him.'

'Sorry,' I said shortly, 'but Gabriel and I are already booked for next Saturday. In fact we're booked every Saturday from now on.'

'Why, what are you doing?'

'I told you, we have these special evenings at home.'

'With your lodgers? God, how boring.' She jerked her head at Matthew, who still had his nose inside the book. 'Will he be there too?'

'I expect so.'

Matthew looked up. 'Wouldn't miss it for the worlds.'

Victoria flounced off.

On the way home from school I spotted Uncle Pat weaving along the pavement with his rolling sailor's gait. He lurched to avoid a passer-by and narrowly missed a lamppost. With a groan I chased after him. 'Uncle Pat . . . !'

'Hello there, Rosie!'

Clouds of boozy breath wafted in my direction. 'Uncle Pat,' I said sternly, tucking my hand through his arm. 'You're useless. I asked you to come here because I needed someone to turn to, but all you do is make for the nearest pub.'

'Oh, Rosie.' Sadly he patted my hand. 'I'm sorry,

truly I am. To tell the truth, it's all come as a bit of a shock to me system.'

I suggested we sit in the park for a while, thinking this would give him time to sober up before he had to face Ma.

'Uncle Pat,' I said, when we had found a bench, 'do you think Dad's still alive?'

'When we were lads, playing around the docks in Liverpool, it always seemed as if Dermot was immortal. He took more risks than the rest of us, and was the only one never to get caught. No . . .' He shook his head. 'No, Dermot's a survivor.'

'Then why doesn't he come home?'

'I don't doubt he has his reasons.' He sighed wheezily. 'I'm not being much help to you, am I – or to your Ma?'

It was Ma he wanted to talk about, mostly.

'I can't get over the change in her, Rosie. She used to be so strong, so outspoken. No frills, no pretences. A steamed pudding and custard woman, that was Francesca. Not right for Dermot, and I told him so from the beginning, but he wouldn't listen. He said she was a challenge, so in he wades and next thing you know he has her falling in love with him. By the time he realized his mistake it was too late and Aisling three months on the way.'

This shocked me. I didn't know Ma was pregnant when she married Dad, but it did explain some of the things he used to shout at her when they had a row, about feeling trapped and him not being the settling-down sort. They used to row constantly at one time, but not so much after we moved into my grandmother's house. Dad was quieter then. Perhaps a little too quiet.

'But she was a damn fine woman, for all her sharp tongue,' Uncle Pat went on. 'And I admired her, even though she blamed me for a lot that wasn't my fault. But of course it was no use trying to tell her that. She didn't want to know.' He sighed again. 'She had to find excuses for him, you see. She always had to find excuses.'

I stared at the bare outline of trees, only just visible in the gathering dusk. 'Do you think that's what she's doing now – finding excuses?'

'Maybe. But I'll tell you something, Rosie. I'd give anything to see her the way she used to be, even if it did mean her bawling me out of the house and throwing me luggage after me. This woman she is now, forever apologizing for her lack of brain and searching after something she doesn't understand – this isn't the Francesca Kelly I knew, only her shadow.'

I couldn't argue. What he said was only what I'd been thinking, that Ma seemed strangely unsure of herself, like an actress finding herself in the wrong play. With a sigh I said, 'I think she's out of her depth, Uncle Pat.'

'And she's not the only one. Dermot's disappearance was mystery enough for me. When it comes to messages from other planets...' He shook his head. 'You're right, Rose. I'm no use to you at all.'

He sounded like a broken man.

I got to my feet. 'Let's go home.'

We walked into the kitchen to find Ma talking to Ralph Lehman from next door. 'Ah, there you are, Patrick,' she said. 'Gabriel's been looking for you. He wants to do some work on your back.'

'What kind of work?' he asked apprehensively.

'Same as he did last time, I expect. You want to be cured, don't you?'

He looked offended. 'You think I enjoy being in constant pain?'

'Well, then. He's in the front room.'

Privately I suspected – and suspected Ma also suspected – that Uncle Pat's back wasn't nearly so bad as he made out and that he was only using it as an excuse not to start digging up the garden. So if Gabriel did succeed in curing him it wouldn't necessarily be a miracle. In fact the only miracle would be if Uncle Pat admitted he was cured.

As the door closed behind him, Ralph Lehman turned to me. 'I was just saying to your mother, Rose, long time no see.'

His jokey manner didn't match with his dry-as-dust appearance. He had the same long nose as his sister, the same squirrel eyes, the same short wiry hair. They could easily have been twins, although Ralph was the younger by four years.

Together they ran an antiquarian bookshop in the high street.

'We've been rather busy lately,' I said defensively.

'I expect you have, with all these visitors. Enid and I were saying only last night, it's like living next door to a hotel, watching new faces arrive every day.'

'We haven't been making too much noise?' Ma looked anxious.

'Oh, just a teeny bit more traffic up and down the stairs, that's all. We've no complaints. You know us, we're not difficult neighbours.' He picked up a cup from the table. 'I must away or Enid will be champing at the bit. 'Byee.'

When he had gone I asked Ma, 'What did he come for?'

'Some flour. Enid's making scones.'

'Of all the feeble excuses! You realize this means they're suspicious. If he discovers we're running a community –'

'Rose, you worry too much about what people think. Your father never cared for anyone's opinion but his own.'

'You did, though,' I reminded her. 'You used to care a lot.'

'That was in the old days,' she said flatly. 'I'm trying to be different now.'

'You have to be yourself, Ma. Dad wouldn't want you any different.'

She turned away to the sink. 'If I'd been different,' she muttered, 'he might never have left me.'

I couldn't bear to listen to this, but when I made for the door she called me back. 'Rose, there's something I have to tell you.'

Reluctantly I turned around.

'The fact is,' she said awkwardly, 'Gabriel's worried about you.'

'About *me*?'

'He's afraid your attitude may be getting in the way.'

'In the way of what?'

She avoided my eyes. 'Our communications. A sceptical presence is bound to make things difficult. That's why he thinks it might be better if you and Matthew didn't come to our meetings for a while.'

'But that's not fair!' I protested. 'Okay, it's true that Matthew's pretty sceptical, but I'm doing my best to keep an open mind.'

She relented a little. 'It's only for a while. Until you both come round to our way of thinking.'

I resented that word 'our'. It made me feel excluded. I said grimly, 'I'm going to talk to Gabriel.'

'Not now, while he's attending to Patrick.'

'Okay, I'll wait outside the door.'

Waiting gave me time to work out what I wanted to say, and when Gabriel finally emerged from the front room I launched into the attack. 'What do you mean by telling Ma I'm not to—'

'Sssh!' He pointed to Uncle Pat, asleep in the chair. 'You see? The treatment has left him totally relaxed. When he wakes up the pain will be gone.'

It seemed to me that Uncle Pat's state of extreme relaxation owed less to Gabriel's treatment than to the amount of whisky he had consumed. 'Gabriel, this is important...'

'Yes, I know. You're upset by what your mother has just told you. Let's go up to your room. We can talk privately there.'

His hand propelled me firmly up the stairs.

9

As soon as we reached the attic I wheeled round on him. 'You can't stop me coming to meetings. I *have* to come, otherwise I shan't know what's going on.'

'Calm down, Rose.' His tone was tolerant, almost indulgent. 'Do I take it, then, you still want to be part of the community?'

'You know I do!'

'Even though you don't really believe in what we're trying to achieve?'

'No. I mean yes...' Driven by despair and anger, I blurted out, 'I'm not the only one who has doubts, you know. Aisling doesn't believe in it either. She warned me not to take it too seriously.'

Anger flared in his eyes, so fiercely that I took a step backwards. 'In that case,' he snapped, 'there doesn't seem much point in your coming to our meetings.'

Or Aisling either. But he didn't say that.

I took a deep breath to steady myself. 'Gabriel, I'm

74

worried. You know Ma hasn't been herself since Dad disappeared. When she first started having these delusions – '

'Delusions?' He picked up the word swiftly, a chill in his voice.

'Aisling persuaded me we should go along with them, but just lately things seem to be getting out of hand. I can't help feeling that to encourage Ma like this is dangerous . . .' My voice trailed off at the sight of his face.

Then, miraculously, his expression changed. He smiled and shook his head. 'Oh, Rose, Rose. Why can't you trust me? I know what I'm doing, I promise you. Come here.'

Half-hypnotized, I took a step towards him. He beckoned me even closer until we were practically touching, nose to chest. My nose, his chest. His skin gave off a radiant warmth through the thinness of his shirt. I felt confused and suddenly breathless.

'Rose, you're full of energy, did you know that? I can feel the force of it from here. It's a powerful gift, you know. If you could only learn how to use it properly you'd be a wonderful asset to the community.'

No one had ever remarked on my energy before. In fact my P.E. teacher once wrote on my report that I was listless and apathetic about all forms of physical exercise. But I was so mesmerized by Gabriel's eyes, boring into mine like twin blue lasers, that I seemed to have stopped breathing. Time had stopped. The earth had stopped. We were suspended, Gabriel and I, in endless, limitless space.

Abruptly he turned away, as if he had lost interest. After a moment I started to breathe again, the floor felt firmer beneath my feet. I saw him staring up at the skylight and actually heard myself say, in quite a normal voice, 'That's where Dad used to observe through his telescope.'

He gave no sign that he had even heard me.

'Although,' I continued, 'when he wanted to use it properly he took it on to the Common to avoid the light pollution.'

He remained silent, but went on staring.

I sank on to the bed and sat cross-legged, trying to appear casual. 'Did you know that Dad was writing a book about Venus?'

Ah, that made him look at me! 'No, I didn't. Do you have a copy?'

'Over there. That A4 notepad on the shelf. He'd been writing it for months.'

He picked up Dad's manuscript and started to read.

'You won't find it easy,' I warned. 'His writing's terrible. But it's all there, every single theory he had about the universe.'

He went on reading until I grew impatient.

'Take it away with you, if you like,' I said. 'Read it at your leisure.'

'Thanks, I will.' He put the notepad under his arm

and smiled at me. 'Well, Rose. Shall we give you one more chance?'

'Yes, please.' My voice sounded small and be-seeching.

'Good girl.' He dropped a light kiss on my forehead. Then, while I was still drowning in a sea of new sensations he added, 'But Matthew will have to be told.'

His voice was so gentle that it took a moment for the words to sink in.

'Told?' I struggled to the surface again. 'You mean, that he can't come to any more meetings?'

'More than that. We don't want him here at all.'

'But he's my oldest friend...'

'He's a hostile presence, Rose. He's holding us back. You must tell him next time he comes.'

'But –'

'No argument. That's my only condition.'

He went, leaving me in turmoil.

I was still in turmoil when Matthew walked into the kitchen half an hour before supper. How could I tell him he was forbidden the house? It meant so much to him, coming here, and not only because of Aisling. We were the nearest thing he'd got to a proper family.

But if I wanted to keep going to meetings...

'Hi, Matthew,' I said. 'I – er, we weren't expecting you tonight.'

'I just called in to see if everything's okay?' He

looked inquiringly at Aisling. She and I were the only people in the kitchen apart from Boris, who was waiting to be fed.

Aisling didn't answer, except to slam a pan of water on the stove. Her temper had been foul lately.

'Everything's fine,' I snapped, guilt making me defensive. 'Why shouldn't it be?'

He raised his eyebrows. 'Plenty of reasons, I'd have thought. I mean, things are hardly normal around here.'

At that moment the door opened and Gabriel walked in, carrying Dad's manuscript. He pulled out a chair and sat down, looking totally at ease. 'Well, Rose? Have you told him?'

'Not yet,' I mumbled.

'Told me what?' demanded Matthew.

Gabriel looked at me expectantly.

'Um, it's nothing personal, Matthew. Just that well, Gabriel doesn't want you to come here any more.' I tried to keep all expression out of my voice. 'He thinks you're a hostile presence.'

Aisling swung round to stare at me.

'I'm not hostile,' Matthew protested. 'Merely curious. It's true I'm inclined to be sceptical . . .'

'That's the problem,' Gabriel intercepted smoothly. 'Sceptics are inevitably limited in their vision. They're incapable of making that giant leap into the unknown, which means they put a brake on the rest of us.'

'And a good thing too!' Matthew flushed with

indignation. 'Somebody has to put the brake on sometime.'

'I agree,' said Aisling. 'Why shouldn't Matthew come to our meetings if he wants to? He's not doing any harm.'

'That's a matter of opinion.' Gabriel shot her a quelling look. 'In any case, I think it should be Rose who makes the decision. After all, it was she who invited him here.' He smiled at me, clearly confident I would do as he commanded.

'It's not Rose's decision at all,' Aisling retorted. 'Matthew's a friend of the family. I'm sure Ma wouldn't want him banned from the house.'

Her championship was so unexpected that Matthew's flush turned from indignation to pleasure. He gazed at her, eyes glowing with gratitude, like a dog who's just been thrown a whole leg of lamb instead of his usual bone.

A small muscle ticked in Gabriel's temple. 'You're overreacting, Aisling.'

'I don't think so. Who are you to say whether people can come here or not? If it's anyone's decision it should be Ma's. So why don't we ask her?'

He said coldly, 'There's no need to trouble your mother. If you're so keen for Matthew to come to our meetings, that's all right with me. It's not worth making a fuss about.' He opened Dad's notepad and started to read.

Matthew said, with dignity, 'Thanks, Aisling.'

'Don't take it personally, wimpo. It's a matter of

principle, that's all.' Removing her apron, she took Ma's waterproof off the hook and pulled on her boots. 'I'm going out.'

'What about supper?' I asked.

'When the water comes to the boil shove in the spuds and turn down the heat. The casserole's in the oven.'

The back door slammed behind her.

There was a silence. I felt too embarrassed to look at Matthew and Gabriel appeared deeply absorbed in Dad's manuscript.

Matthew cleared his throat. 'I'd better go.'

I accompanied him into the hall. Still feeling awkward I said, quite truthfully, 'I'm glad Aisling won. I didn't really want to ban you from meetings.'

'You'd have done it though, wouldn't you, just because he told you to?'

'No, I wouldn't.' But my voice gave me away.

He sighed. 'Your trouble is you're in thrall to that guy.'

This remark struck me so forcibly that I was silent for several seconds, thinking about it. Was I in thrall to Gabriel? To be honest, I wasn't entirely sure what it meant.

Matthew added smugly, 'Anyway, I've got him worried now. He knows I'm on to him. That's why he wanted to throw me out.' He opened the front door. 'Doesn't it strike you as odd that we hear all this talk about saving the planet, yet so far nobody's suggested taking any action? Isn't it time we started doing something practical, like saving energy? Or banning pesticides? Or going out and trying to convert other people to a different way of thinking?'

'Ma did say, right at the beginning, that we had to be self-sufficient.'

'Self-supporting, not self-sufficient. There's a difference, you know. Or are you too besotted to see it?'

He was beginning to annoy me. Sarcastically I said, 'I take it you'll be coming next Saturday, then?'

'Of course. Aisling wants me there. You heard what she said.'

I slammed the door behind him and returned to the kitchen, only to find that Gabriel too had disappeared. He must have gone out of the back door, because he certainly hadn't come through the hall. What's more, he'd taken Dad's manuscript with him.

Later that night, when everyone had gone to bed, I crept down to the front room and looked up a word in the dictionary. The definition said:

> **thrall (-awl, n., a., and v.t. (1) Slave (of, to, person or thing, lit. & fig.); bondage: (2) adj. Enslaved (to); (3) v.t. Enslave. Hence thraldom.**

I put the dictionary back on the shelf. Enslaved, was I? Well, perhaps. Just a little.

10

On Saturday morning I knocked on the door of the room Uncle Pat shared with Gabriel. There was no answer, but then it was only ten-thirty and I knew Uncle Pat would still be asleep, so I went in anyway.

This was the first time I'd seen it since they started sharing and I was interested to note that the room had been divided into two narrow cells by a line of furniture down the middle. There was a wardrobe opening on to Gabriel's half and a chest-of-drawers opening on to Uncle Pat's; then two chairs, one facing one way and one the other, like in a game of musical chairs. Gabriel's half was fanatically neat and tidy; Uncle Pat's looked like a jumble sale.

I approached the mound of bedclothes and gave it a push. It stirred and snorted and moved around a bit, but no face appeared.

'Uncle Pat, wake up.' I seized what I hoped was his shoulder and gave it a shake. 'Ma wants you.'

'Wa?'

'She's going to the supermarket and needs you to help carry the heavy things.'

He struggled to sit up, his chest bare, his hair in wispy disarray. 'What about me back?'

'There's nothing wrong with your back,' I said firmly. 'Hurry up, she's waiting for you.'

'Saints!' He stuck out his tongue and tried to see it out of the corner of his eye. 'I've a mouth like a cat's litter-box. Any chance of a cuppa?'

'Only if you come downstairs.'

'Ah, but you're a hard woman, Rosie. You take after your mother in that respect. Or rather the woman your mother used to be, before she changed into a blancmange.'

I sat on the chair that faced his half of the room. 'It seems to me, Uncle Pat, you're getting on a lot better with Ma now than you ever did in the old days. I'd have thought you'd be glad she's changed.'

Sadly he shook his head. 'I'd sooner have her the way she used to be, with a bit of fire in her soul. All this "Please, Patrick" and "Thank you kindly, Patrick" and "if you'd be so good, Patrick" is beginning to give me the pip.'

'She's coming to rely on you, though. And I think she'd trust you even more if you didn't keep going on binges.'

He sighed. 'Sorry, Rosie, but the way things are in this house drives me to it. I doubt if I can stand much more community living. I'm not cut out for it.'

'Is that why you put up the barricade?' I asked, looking at the line of furniture.

'His Lordship's idea, not mine.'

'What does he keep in the wardrobe? He doesn't have any clothes, except what Ma's given him.'

'Don't ask me. It's locked and he's taken the key.' Uncle Pat threw back the bedclothes, revealing – to my relief – that he slept in striped pyjama bottoms. 'Now if you'll kindly leave, Rosie, I'll get meself ready to go out with your mother.'

Downstairs I found Ma in the kitchen, already wearing her coat. I told her Uncle Pat was coming and she nodded absently, checking through her shopping list.

'Ma,' I said, 'do you approve of Uncle Pat more than you used to?'

She looked surprised. 'I like him well enough. Provided, that is, he stays off the bottle.'

Encouraged, I persisted, 'He's very like Dad in some ways, isn't he? Except he's not so handsome.'

'Oh, Patrick's well enough in his own style.' She sniffed. 'That's the trouble with the Irish, they don't need to rely on looks. They can charm themselves into anything, if they've a mind to.'

'You're not sorry he came, then?'

'It was a shock at the time, I won't deny it. But on the whole it's worked out better than I expected.'

Gabriel strolled into the kitchen. When he saw Ma in her coat he said, 'You're going out, Francesca?'

She nodded. 'I want to start shopping for the Christmas food. I can't bear leaving it till the last minute and anyway I'll need to get plenty in if there's to be six of us.'

'At least,' said Gabriel.

Ma looked puzzled. 'You think there'll be more?'

'It's possible.'

'Well, I suppose Matthew may join us on Boxing Day, but he's bound to have Christmas dinner with his mother...'

'I don't mean Matthew.'

Ma stared at Gabriel. He smiled.

She said faintly, 'In that case I'd better order a bigger bird.'

'It might be wise.'

She went into the hall. 'Patrick, are you ready?'

'Sure I am.' He stumbled downstairs, still doing up the front of his trousers.

'You look terrible! I'm not walking through the streets with an unshaven man at this hour of the morning – and by the smell of you, unwashed as well.'

He grinned at her, unrepentant. 'Don't worry, Fran. I'll push me little wire trolley two paces behind so everyone will know I'm only the porter.'

Ma opened her mouth as if to snap back at him, then caught sight of Gabriel in the doorway. 'Don't be silly, Patrick,' she said mildly. 'There's no need for that. Best put on your coat, there's a cold wind blowing.'

85

The gleam in Uncle Pat's eyes slowly died. As he followed her through the door he looked at me with a hopeless shrug of his shoulders.

'Why did you tell Ma there might be more of us for Christmas?' I asked Gabriel. 'Are you expecting someone?'

He gave me an intent, speculative look. 'Can I trust you, Rose?'

How could he even ask? I put everything I'd got into saying, 'You know you can!'

'In that case I'll be frank with you. I'm getting a little worried about the community. Just lately there's been a falling-off of enthusiasm, have you noticed?'

I shook my head, unwilling to commit myself.

'Even your mother seems more concerned with worldly matters. The problem is we're building on shaky foundations. Too many old people. What we need is some younger blood...'

He seemed to be thinking aloud. I stared at him, mesmerized.

'So far, Rose, you've not had much chance to show us what you can do, have you? Perhaps the time has come to give you that chance. It would mean putting those powers of yours to the test. Are you ready for that, do you think?'

'I – I don't understand...'

'You will, Rose.' He looked at me gravely, waves of magnetism flowing in my direction. 'Tonight you'll understand everything.'

* * *

By the time the meeting started I'd worked myself into a state of acute nervous tension, made worse when Ma announced she'd had another message. We were to prepare ourselves, she said, for something momentous.

We were seated round the candle as usual, Aisling in her catsuit, Aunt Eunice with her knickers showing and Matthew yearning after Aisling. It was Uncle Pat, perched precariously on his stool, who asked the question I was dying to ask but dared not in case I got accused of being sceptical.

'How exactly did the message get here, Fran?'

Ma gave him a frosty look. 'Well, it didn't come by second class mail, Patrick, that's for sure.'

He grinned, clearly delighted by this flash of her old spirit. 'It's just that you said the wineglass method was too slow, so I wondered how –'

'I gave the message to Francesca,' Gabriel said smoothly, 'but I don't intend to waste time on unnecessary explanations. It's far more important we should prepare ourselves for this coming event. Last week, for example, we talked about our problems. Tonight we shall discuss how we can overcome these problems and turn our weaknesses into strengths.'

This was something of an anti-climax. I felt relieved, yet at the same time disappointed.

'We'll start with Eunice,' he said.

Aunt Eunice looked startled. 'But I don't have a problem any more. You said –'

'We agreed you're no longer alone. However it seems to me you have a greater enemy, one that often prevents you doing what you would like to do.' The blue of his eyes was electric. 'That enemy is fear.'

Her mouth dropped open. 'But how –?'

'You must conquer it, Eunice. You must look your fear in the face and destroy it. Do you know how that can be done?'

Speechless, she shook her head.

'Later I will show you. Now, Patrick –'

'Me back's better. It's miles better. Watch...' Uncle Pat slid off the stool, wincing as his bottom hit the floor, and looked triumphantly at Gabriel.

'There's nothing wrong with your back, Patrick. It's the drink you have to beat.'

I began to feel uncomfortable. He was going for the jugular and it scared me. Uncle Pat scowled furiously and even Ma looked nervous.

'What about me?' Aisling demanded, as if to draw his fire away from the others. 'How can I overcome *my* weakness?'

Gabriel frowned. 'I thought you didn't have one.'

'So did I, but now I'm beginning to wonder.'

'Okay, so what's the problem?'

'You tell me.'

They glared at each other, eyes locked. This made me uneasy. Frankly I preferred it when they ignored each other.

Gabriel said coolly, 'I think you need to give more thought to this question, Aisling. We'll discuss it another time. Now, Rose...' He turned to me, ignoring Matthew as if to make it clear he was only there under sufferance. 'Come and sit here, in front of me.'

I shuffled ungracefully across the floor, bracing myself to declare my problems, which were now so numerous I didn't know where to begin. Boris, crouched at Gabriel's side, opened his eyes to stare at me contemptuously, then closed them again.

'Take my hands,' Gabriel commanded.

I clasped his outstretched hands and gazed into his eyes. They were like brilliant blue stones, strangely unwinking. My own ached with the effort not to blink.

'Are you concentrating, Rose?'

I nodded.

'Good girl. Now I want everyone to keep absolutely still. Rose is about to use her remarkable store of energy on our behalf.'

There he went again, raving about my energy. It was true I could feel a tingling sensation where Gabriel's hands touched mine, but it seemed to me this was due to something entirely different...

'Rose,' he said quietly. 'Concentrate.'

I concentrated.

Very softly a sound crept into the room, a delicate eerie twanging, like a lute.

'Do you hear?' asked Gabriel. 'Beautiful, isn't it? Some people call it the music of the spheres. Listen again.'

It was getting louder. Not just a lute, but several other instruments I couldn't for the moment identify. They weren't playing a recognizable tune, but kept repeating the same plaintive, haunting phrase that seemed about to resolve itself into a melody only to change its mind at the last minute.

'It's a synthesizer,' Matthew stated. 'And it's coming from upstairs.'

Gabriel asked coldly, 'How am I supposed to be working it – by remote control?'

Matthew flushed but stuck to his guns. 'It's not impossible.'

Instinctively I glanced up at the ceiling. The room directly above was the one shared by Gabriel and Uncle Pat. But we were all here, there wasn't anyone missing; and Gabriel's hands still held mine, so he couldn't possibly be manipulating anything.

He said, 'Go ahead and look, Matthew, if you want.'

Matthew shrugged. 'It's stopped.'

So it had. Gabriel said with a sigh, 'It must have sensed hostility in the atmosphere.'

'It wasn't very tuneful anyway,' Aunt Eunice remarked.

'Can't stand that modern stuff,' Uncle Pat agreed. 'I like something you can sing along to, with a good rousing chorus.'

So far Ma hadn't said a word and I dared not look round to see her reaction.

Gabriel's grip tightened on my fingers. 'We haven't

finished yet.' He lowered his voice, speaking only to me. 'Now Rose, remember what I told you. I'm giving you a chance to show what you can do. Try to concentrate hard.'

He was hypnotizing me again. I could see the candle flame reflected in his eyes, two tiny flickering fires.

A definite bump came from upstairs.

There *is* someone up there!' Matthew exclaimed.

Aunt Eunice clutched her throat. Uncle Pat tried to stand up but Gabriel put out a hand to stop him. We all sat there, straining our ears, and I could only think, *This has nothing to do with me. No matter what he says, I'm not doing this thing*.

The stairs creaked.

Uncle Pat swore under his breath and Aunt Eunice gave a little whimper. I tore my eyes from Gabriel's to look at the door.

It opened slowly.

Two figures stood there. I say 'figures' because it was impossible to tell whether they were male or female. They also appeared unnaturally tall, though this may have been because the rest of us were sitting on the floor. They were dressed in identical black leather jump suits and their hair, lit by the hall lamp behind them, was a fiery red.

'Welcome,' said Gabriel.

At that point the candle went out, extinguished by the draught from the door.

11

Their names were Zak and Jedda.

Thirty minutes later they sat with the rest of us round the kitchen table, drinking cocoa. Normal as this may seem, it was the only reassuring thing about them so far. From the moment they had materialized in the doorway I had been conscious of a deep unease.

Zak's voice was definitely masculine, but he spoke with a strange, clipped accent. So far Jedda had not spoken at all, but somehow she gave the impression of being a girl although there was nothing about her appearance to suggest it, not even a hint of bosom. Both had deathly pale faces with black eyebrows and bloodless lips. They had not said where they came from and Gabriel hadn't asked. He had done most of the talking. That was how we knew what their names were and that they liked cocoa. Matthew stared at them with obvious suspicion, Uncle Pat kept muttering under his breath, Aunt Eunice looked scared out of her wits and Boris had taken refuge on top of the fridge.

Aisling sat with a face like stone, saying nothing.

Ma, in a desperate attempt to make everything seem commonplace, was trying to sort out the sleeping arrangements. 'That's agreed, then. Jedda comes in with me and Zak can have the folding bed in Gabriel and Patrick's room.'

'His side,' growled Uncle Pat, jerking his head at Gabriel.

'I don't want to share,' Aunt Eunice said in a quavery voice. 'You shouldn't make me share, not at my age. This was my sister's home.'

'We've been through all that, Aunt,' Ma said wearily. 'You don't have to share with anyone.'

'It's getting too crowded.' Aunt Eunice darted a fearful glance at Zak and Jedda. 'It never used to be so crowded in the old days.'

'We're a community, Eunice.' Gabriel leaned forward to gaze directly into her face. 'And you must – stop – worrying. I made you a promise, didn't I? Tomorrow I will show you what to do.'

'Yes,' she said faintly, staring back at him. 'Tomorrow.'

He stood up and turned to Ma. 'Patrick and I will see to the beds, Francesca.'

Uncle Pat muttered something about his back, but he got to his feet all the same. With bad grace he said to Zak, 'If you fetch your luggage I'll show you where to put it.'

'We have no luggage,' said Zak.

Everyone stared. 'Not even a toothbrush?' Aunt Eunice enquired in a shocked voice.

Zak asked, 'What's a toothbrush?'

I wondered if perhaps Venusians didn't have teeth – since neither of them had smiled it was impossible to tell – or whether all that sulphur in the atmosphere made them so perfect they didn't have to brush them, ever.

Gabriel said, 'Come with me,' and led them out of the kitchen.

Uncle Pat followed, muttering to me out of the corner of his mouth, 'Don't worry, I'll keep my eye on 'em.'

Aunt Eunice lifted Boris down from the fridge and hugged him tightly – not so much for his reassurance, I suspected, as for her own. 'All that talk about bedrooms . . . now I can't remember where I'm supposed to sleep.'

'I'll show you, Aunt.' Aisling, still stony-faced, took her from the room.

This left Ma, Matthew and me. Under cover of washing the cocoa mugs I said, 'Ma, are you sure you don't mind sharing with that girl? She's very strange looking.'

She rested her hands on the sink. 'Really, Rose. What harm do you imagine will come to me?'

In my mind's eye I saw Ma asleep in bed, Jedda bending over her, and it was such a vision of menace that I shuddered.

'Anyway,' she continued, stiffening her spine, 'this

means the community's now complete. Everyone's arrived, exactly as your father said they would.'

I caught Matthew's eye. He was about to say something tactless, I could tell, so I dropped the tea cloth and pushed him out of the room.

As soon as we'd reached the hall he said, 'I never saw such a pair of phoneys! Their names, for a start. Every science fiction book ever written has a character called Zak.' He laughed shortly. 'Of course it was them operating the synthesizer.'

I couldn't stop shivering. 'But how could they get into the house? We'd have heard them go upstairs.'

'They could have come through the skylight.'

'You mean dropped from the sky?' I raised my eyebrows. 'And I thought you were supposed to be the sceptical one!'

'That's not what I meant and you know it,' he snapped. 'If there's one thing I'm bloody sure of it's that they haven't come from Venus.'

Matthew didn't often swear. He regarded it as juvenile. Which only proved how disturbed he felt.

He went on, 'Gabriel wasn't at all surprised to see them, did you notice?'

'Why should he be? He'd already told Ma to buy in more food for Christmas.'

'Which suggests it was fixed. And did you see Aisling's face? She was furious. When Gabriel said "Welcome" she threw him a look that would stun a police dog at fifty metres.'

Trust Matthew to have been looking at Aisling.

'What's strange about that?' I demanded. 'She's never liked him.'

'Rose, you're an idiot.'

'Thanks, Matthew.' Pointedly I opened the front door. Halfway out he hesitated. 'I don't trust those two jokers. If you take my advice you'll keep them out of your mother's way. Something like this could easily tip her over the edge.'

This was too close to my own fears for comfort. Suppressing them, I said, 'Hasn't it occurred to you that *she* may be the sane one, far saner than the rest of us?'

He sucked in his breath. 'If you think that you must be in an even worse state of delusion than I'd realized. In my opinion she's badly in need of counselling.'

'If this is delusion, Matthew, then it's getting to be delusion on the grand scale. There's no counsellor been born yet who could cure what's going on in our house.' I pushed him further out of the door. 'And if you can't see it for yourself then you'd better stop coming here.'

'You don't mean that?'

'Yes, I do.' Now that I'd said it I realized I couldn't take it back. Anyway, he made me so mad I didn't *want* to take it back. It was only the hurt look on his face that made me add, 'Till after Christmas, anyway.'

'But that's two weeks away. A lot can happen in two weeks.' His voice was doom-laden.

'Yes, it can. That means we'll have plenty to talk about next time we meet. Good*night*, Matthew.' I closed the door behind him and turned around to see Gabriel leaning against the newel post.

'Good girl,' he said, smiling.

I mumbled awkwardly, 'There's so many of us now, we've enough to feed without Matthew as well.'

'Quite right.' He came nearer and lightly dropped a kiss on my forehead, my reward for doing as I was told. 'I'm pleased with you, Rose.'

As he started up the stairs I called after him, 'Gabriel . . .'

He paused. 'Yes?'

'Who are they?'

He did not pretend to misunderstand. 'Friends of mine.'

'They don't look like you.'

'Any reason why they should?'

'I suppose not. But where do they come from?'

'The same place I do, Rose. A long way off, beyond your wildest imaginings. One day, if you continue to be good, I may take you there.'

'Oh. Thanks.'

That night, as I paid my final visit to the bathroom, I bumped into Jedda coming out. She was still wearing her jump suit and I wondered if she intended to sleep in it. 'Okay?' I inquired, not so much to be polite as to force her to speak.

'Ya.' She slid past me and disappeared into Ma's room.

Could 'ya' be Venusian for 'yes'?

Aisling was asleep by the time I was ready for bed.

At least, she had buried her head under the quilt and didn't answer when I called her name. Taking care not to disturb her, I stood on my bed to inspect the skylight. It was closed but the catch was unfastened. We never left it open, there were too many burglaries around this area. I fixed the catch, got into bed and slid beneath the sheets.

Young blood, Gabriel had said. *The community needs young blood* . . .

What if Matthew's theory was right? Could they have climbed on to the roof and let themselves in through the skylight? They were certainly dressed for such an exercise. And if Gabriel had sneaked up to the attic earlier and left the skylight open . . .

But that would suggest the whole thing had been planned as a sort of interstellar confidence trick, which I couldn't accept. I was prepared to believe there might be some connection between their arrival and the music we'd heard, but the explanation couldn't possibly be as simple as the one Matthew had put forward. After all, Uncle Pat shared that room with Gabriel, even if it was divided down the middle. Surely he'd have noticed if there was a synthesizer around, or even a tape recorder?

Unless Gabriel had already hidden one in the wardrobe? That might explain why he kept it locked.

Just before dropping off to sleep I heard crying and lifted my head from the pillow. 'Aisling?'

She didn't answer. The crying stopped.

Uneasily I drifted into sleep.

12

There was a queue at the post office – the usual pre-Christmas rush for stamps – and two places ahead of me Enid Lehman was talking over her shoulder to someone I didn't recognize. She hadn't seen me, that was obvious from the things she said.

'. . . and as for the latest arrivals – my dear, they're like something out of a horror film. I can't think what Francesca's playing at. Mind you, I suspect she may be short of cash. Not that Dermot exactly pulled his weight in that direction, but –'

She'd spotted me. Suddenly her eyes glazed over and she opened and shut her mouth like a landed fish.

The other woman murmured something about lowering the tone of the neighbourhood before Enid nudged her furiously and waved. 'Hello, Rose. Everything all right?'

'Fine,' I assured her, as anxious as she was to pretend I was stone deaf.

The truth was that things had gone downhill badly

since Zak and Jedda arrived. A week ago Gabriel had stepped up our meetings to one every other night – Matthew would be livid if he knew what he was missing – and last night's had been like a group therapy session, with Gabriel ordering us to tell each other what our worst faults were. He told Ma to start, as he always did, and for a long time she havered, looking unhappy. Eventually she said she wished that Aisling weren't so secretive and that I didn't care so much about what other people thought. I was amazed. If I were asked to make a list of my own ten worst faults this would definitely not be among them. The ten most trivial maybe, but not the ten worst. Then she said she wished Aunt Eunice wouldn't take out her back teeth in the evenings and stuff them down the side of the sofa, whereupon Aunt Eunice burst into tears and the session ended.

Lately Uncle Pat had taken to staying in bed most of the day and I could get no sense out of him at all. He said he'd tried to force open the wardrobe to see if there was a tape recorder hidden inside, but Gabriel came in and caught him so he had to pretend he was drunk and didn't know where he was. I asked what happened at night, with him and Gabriel and Zak sleeping in the same room, and he said nothing happened except that one of them snored and he thought it was Zak. This reassured me somewhat. Snoring seemed such an earthbound activity.

When I left the post office I went into town to do my

Christmas shopping. The trouble was that at home it didn't feel like Christmas, even though Ma had put up the decorations as usual with Uncle Pat's help. But it wasn't the same without Matthew and I began to wish I hadn't asked him to stay away. To make up for my meanness I bought him an extra-nice present, a book about molecular structure, very glossy and full of diagrams, which cost a bomb.

The shops were full of normal people buying normal presents for other normal people, which I found very soothing in my present state of mind. In Boots I was squirting *Poison* on my wrist from a tester, with a view to choosing Aisling's present, when a voice behind me said, 'Hi, Rose. They've let you out, then?'

I turned to see Victoria. She was wearing a long black coat, knee-length boots and so much eye make-up it was a wonder she could see where she was going. This was the first time we had met since term ended five days ago.

'Hi,' I said. 'Who's let me out?'

'Those people you live with. Your community.'

I stared at her. 'Who told you about the community?'

'I met Matthew. He says it's weird. He says it's really taken your family over.'

I could have killed Matthew. I wished now I hadn't spent so much money on his present. How dare he tell Victoria!

How *much* had he told Victoria?

She put her arm through mine, confidentially. 'Let's go for a Coke. I've missed you, Rose. We don't seem to have talked properly for ages. You must tell me *everything*.'

Reluctantly I let her drag me off to the nearest snack bar.

As soon as we had found a corner seat and sat down with our Cokes she started grilling me about Gabriel. It soon became clear that Matthew had told her very little, only that he didn't trust Gabriel or his two weird friends and feared they might take advantage of Ma's hospitality. I said offhandedly, 'You don't want to take too much notice of Matthew. He only says those things because he's jealous.'

'Jealous of Gabriel?'

'I'm afraid so, yes.' No need to specify that his jealousy was on account of Aisling, not me.

'Does he have reason to be?'

'Hardly!' I felt pleased with the way my voice sounded when I said this – amused, with just the right degree of boredom. 'He's not even in the same league.'

Her eyes gleamed. 'You mean – as a kisser?'

Luckily I didn't have to answer because I was too busy choking over my Coke. When I'd recovered I said, 'So what's been happening in *your* life lately? Have you been out with that boy you went to the party with? Sorry, I forget his name.'

'Shane.' She was easily diverted. 'Actually we've been seeing quite a lot of each other. Wait, I've got a photo.' She rummaged in her bag. 'There! Don't you think he's gorgeous?'

He looked pretty run-of-the-mill to me, except for a pair of enormous ears. With ears like those he should grow his hair down to his shoulders, not cut short like a lavatory brush.

'Anyway,' she went on, putting the photograph away, 'things have moved pretty fast since the party.'

'How fast?'

'I'm not sure I should tell you. You might be shocked.' She gave me a considering look, her head on one side. 'First tell me how far things have gone between you and Gabriel.'

'Er – pretty far.'

'Farther than kissing?'

It was no use, I couldn't bring myself to tell an outright lie. 'Not yet, no.'

She heaved a romantic sigh. 'Shane's a wonderful kisser.'

'So's Gabriel.' Which was something of an exaggeration, but not outright perjury.

To be honest, I was beginning to have mixed feelings about Gabriel. It was true I found him wildly attractive, but he also frightened me a bit. Things had changed since the arrival of Zak and Jedda. Only that morning, in the hallway, I had come across what was clearly an incident. Zak had Aunt Eunice trapped against the wall, his outstretched arms on either side of her head and his face pushed intimidatingly close to hers. She looked terrified.

'Leave her alone, you great bully!' I yelled. 'Only cowards threaten defenceless old ladies.'

He wheeled round on me, eyes blazing, and I was so unnerved that I took a step backwards. Then he smiled, which was even more frightening, and swung his hand back as if to hit me. But at that moment the kitchen door opened and Gabriel appeared, demanding to know what was going on.

For about three seconds they had squared up to each other, eyeball to eyeball. Eventually Gabriel's eyeballs won and Zak slunk away upstairs, muttering something venomous under his breath. Then Gabriel turned to Aunt Eunice, who was quietly whimpering in the corner, and said, 'Eunice, the time has come.'

And she had gone off with him, still whimpering, into the dining room. Since then there had been an atmosphere of menace in the house and it affected everything, even my feelings towards Gabriel. But of course I couldn't explain any of this to Victoria. The gulf between us seemed to be widening all the time.

She said, her eyes fixed on my face, 'I'd love to come to one of your meetings.'

I came back to the present with a jolt. 'What?'

'They sound so interesting. Perhaps I could join your community? I expect you need new members.'

'Sorry,' I said shortly. 'The list is closed. Anyway, you don't even know what the community's about.'

'How can I, unless I come?' Her expression was guileless, pleading. 'Go on, Rose. Let me come, just once. I promise I'll be good.'

'I – er, I'll have to ask Gabriel.'

'Thanks!'

Obviously she regarded it as good as done. We finished our drinks, which Victoria insisted on paying for, and she breezed off.

I arrived home to find Gabriel giving Aunt Eunice lessons in kung fu.

'I'm learning to defend myself,' she told me. 'Gabriel says it's so I shan't be frightened any more.'

I summoned up the courage to ask Gabriel if he thought this was wise. 'She *is* seventy-two,' I reminded him.

'That's why I'm teaching her the Ving Tsun system, Rose. It's based on economy of movement and therefore doesn't rely on physical strength alone. It couldn't be more suitable for a woman of Eunice's age.'

'It was started by a nun,' Aunt Eunice chipped in. 'Look, Rose – this is what we call the Main Horse Stance...'

She stood with her feet apart and her stockinged toes turned in, both pairs of spectacles swinging on their chains. Her expression was belligerent but blissful.

'Oh, well,' I said helplessly. 'I suppose it can't do any harm.'

Gabriel said, 'On the contrary, Rose, it will do a great deal of good. I promised Eunice I would help her overcome her fear of physical violence. To do that she must feel capable of defending herself in any situation. Besides, it will give her a sense of achievement.'

I left Aunt Eunice attempting to balance on one leg and went into the kitchen to find Aisling ironing a man's shirt.

'Are you aware,' I demanded, 'that we've acquired a martial aunt?'

'I'm aware.' The way she thumped the iron about suggested it was not a task she was enjoying.

'I thought we women didn't have to iron men's shirts now we've been liberated,' I observed. 'Aren't men supposed to iron their own shirts these days?'

Thump, thump.

'Whose is it, anyway?' I inquired. 'Gabriel's or Uncle Pat's?'

'Neither.' She held up the pale blue shirt for me to see. 'Don't you recognize it?'

'It's one of Dad's.'

'Exactly.' She started ironing again. Thump, thump, bang. 'Try to keep a grip on reality, Rose. Gabriel doesn't have any shirts of his own. At least he didn't before he came here. Now he has a whole wardrobeful, thanks to Dad.'

'It's no use getting ratty with me, Aisling. You're the one who said we had to go along with whatever Ma wanted to do. It's not my fault we've got lodgers.'

'Oh no? Who was it sent for Uncle Pat?'

'Okay, okay, I admit it. I sent for him because I was dead worried. I hoped he'd be able to help us. And

106

he has tried,' I added quickly, catching sight of her caustic expression. 'But he says himself that he's out of his depth.'

'We're all out of our depth, beanpole. The question is, why doesn't one of us pull the plug and let the water out?'

I stared at her, unsure what she was getting at. 'I don't know. Could we?'

She rested the iron, looking suddenly weary. 'I'm afraid we may have let it go too far. If only Ma—'

Before she could finish, the door opened and Jedda walked in. 'Oh, hi,' I said brightly, to cover up the awkward pause, but she didn't answer. This was because she had personal stereo cans clamped over her ears. Swaying in rhythm with the music only she could hear, she wandered over to the fridge, opened the door, took out a carton of milk, poured herself a full glass, sipped it and wandered out again without even glancing in our direction.

'Bloody nerve,' Aisling muttered.

'I don't mind *her*,' I said. 'It's *him* I can't stand.'

'I can't stand either of them. The sooner they hightail it out of here the better as far as I'm concerned.'

After a pause I said, 'Aisling, why do you think they came here?'

She shrugged. 'Haven't a clue. Except it's obvious she's got the hots for Gabriel something chronic.'

'Jedda? But I thought she belonged to Zak.'

'That's what Zak thought too. I'm not surprised he's starting to get stroppy.'

'Stroppy' struck me as something of an under-
statement. I watched Aisling fold the ironed shirt
with care, almost reverence. Because it had been
worn by Gabriel? Or because it was Dad's and she
missed him badly?

'Well, whoever they are they have to go,' I said
firmly. 'We have to *make* them go. For Ma's sake. The
longer we let them stay here the worse this whole
situation is likely to get. We've got to tell them.'

'They wouldn't take any notice. Even if we tried to
chuck them out physically they'd only come back.'
She shivered. 'They're like a pair of evil squatters it's
impossible to budge.'

The prospect of being forced to live with Zak and
Jedda for the rest of my life appalled me. 'Then we
must ask Gabriel to tell them,' I said. 'He's the one
who brought them here. It's his responsibility to
make them leave.'

'*You* ask him, Rose. He's far more likely to take
notice of you than he is of me. You're his blue-eyed
girl, the one with all this marvellous energy. Go on,
you ask him.'

'All right, I will!'

As I turned to the door she thrust the shirt into my
arms. 'Here, take this with you. And you can also tell
the Master of the Universe that laundry will be extra
in future.'

Quaking in my moccasins, I carried the shirt
upstairs.

13

The room was empty. Gabriel was still downstairs with Aunt Eunice. As I laid the shirt on the bed I noticed Dad's manuscript lying on the bed and stole a look at the first page. Although I'd read it before it struck me with new force:

> '...then surely it's logical to conclude that other forms of intelligence must be watching us with great interest at this time. I say "at this time" because clearly we have reached a crucial stage in our development, the point of no return; and if we prove incapable of solving our own problems, then these other forms of intelligence – who may indeed have been through a similar crisis in the past – could well decide to intervene, perhaps even take over.'

Take over...?
'Rose?' Gabriel stood in the doorway. I'd been so

absorbed in my reading I hadn't heard him come in.

'Oh, hi,' I said with a guilty start. 'I just brought your shirt up for you. Aisling's ironed it beautifully. Did you finish Dad's book?'

He nodded, his eyes fixed on my face. 'Your father was a man of remarkable vision.'

'Yes, he was.' I had to get this over with, but my knees were literally shaking. 'Gabriel, there's something I have to tell you. About Zak and Jedda. We don't like having them here. That is, Aisling and me. We want them to leave.'

For a moment he looked blank, as if he didn't understand what I was saying. Then he frowned and said, 'Forget about Zak and Jedda. They're not important.'

'But we –'

'I said *forget about Zak and Jedda!*' His eyes flashed with anger, making me quake even more. But then he seemed to recover and went on, quite mildly, 'Rose, you once told me that your father used to take his telescope on to the Common when he wanted to observe the stars. Can you remember where he went? The exact site, I mean.'

'Yes, of course. He took me with him a couple of times.'

'Could you show me?'

I swallowed hard, but dared not refuse. 'Now?'

'As soon as I've changed my shirt.'

He stripped off his T-shirt, revealing a satin smooth brown chest. I became aware that I was staring and started to blush. Luckily Gabriel didn't seem to notice. He reached for the blue shirt Aisling had just ironed and put it on, letting it hang loose over Dad's chinos. Traitorously, it crossed my mind how delightful it would be if we could bump into Victoria, quite by chance.

It was a twenty minute uphill walk to the Common. I was curious to know why Gabriel wanted to visit the site, but felt too intimidated to ask. Perhaps he was hoping to make some observations of his own?

The place where Dad used to set up his telescope was on the highest point, a flat, wide space unobstructed by trees. From here you could see most of the town spread out like a map, with the river snaking through the middle and two church spires pointing towards the sky. Gabriel stared round him with a curiously intent expression. 'Oh, yes,' he murmured. 'Oh, yes!'

'Do you like it?' I inquired. An odd question, but I wasn't sure what we were supposed to be looking for.

'It's not a matter of liking, Rose. It's a matter of whether or not this is the right place.'

'The right place for what?'

'For making contact.' His eyes searched the overcast sky. 'Possibly even for a landing.'

'A *landing*?' My voice squeaked incredulously, I couldn't help it.

'Why not, Rose? Why not?' He started walking rapidly away from me.

Did he seriously expect that some alien spaceship

was going to touch down on this unlikely spot and disgorge a load of eager Venusian tourists? Or was it all part of the mysterious game that Aisling had said he was playing?

But he wasn't playing a game, I felt certain. At the beginning he might have been, but not any longer.

I hurried after him. 'Gabriel! Please, I have to talk to you...'

'Not now, Rose.' He quickened his pace.

'It's no use, I can't keep putting it off. I'm too worried. It's about Ma...'

He stopped and swung round to face me. 'I thought we'd agreed you don't have to worry about your mother. She knows exactly what she's doing – and so do I. You have to trust us, Rose.'

The intensity of his gaze robbed me of all coherent thought. Feebly I said, 'The trouble is, I can't believe –'

'– in the Venus thing. Yes, I know.' Amazingly, he smiled. Put out a hand to stroke my cheek. 'It's all right, Rose. It doesn't matter. All I ask is that you stop worrying. Relax. Trust me.' His finger traced the line of my jaw and ended up resting against my lips. 'Okay?'

Helplessly I nodded.

He took my hand and we walked home like a pair of lovers.

The following evening he started off the meeting by accusing Ma of getting so tied up with Christmas preparations that she was in danger of forgetting our main objective.

'I realize that,' Ma said unhappily. 'But it's Christmas Eve on Thursday and there's still so much to do.'

'Do I detect, Francesca, a lessening in your spirit of dedication?'

'No, of course not. But – well, we do have to carry on with our ordinary lives.' Was there just the faintest hint of rebellion in her tone?

'You can't stop now, Francesca. Having come so far it would be criminal to give up before we achieve our goal.'

'And what goal would that be?' Uncle Pat demanded.

Gabriel ignored him. 'I think we should forget about Christmas.'

Ma's face dropped. 'But I've bought the bird. And Aisling's made a beautiful cake.'

'Birds, cake – this is trivia, Francesca. You really must make an effort to keep your mind on a higher plane. Dermot expects it of you.'

There came a sharp hissing noise. It was Aisling, drawing in her breath. Next moment she got up and marched out of the room. Ma reached out a hand as if to stop her but Gabriel said, 'Let her go. She's no great loss.'

Zak uttered a strange, caustic little laugh. He sat next to Aunt Eunice, who shrank visibly whenever his sleeve brushed her arm. Jedda's gaze was fixed adoringly on Gabriel. Now Aisling had pointed it out

I was surprised I hadn't noticed it before. But then I'd probably been too busy gazing adoringly at him myself.

Ignoring Zak, Gabriel turned his attention back to Ma. 'Did you hear what I said, Francesca? Dermot expects it of you.'

'Baloney,' muttered Uncle Pat. 'Dermot never expected anything of anybody. He took people the way he found them.'

'Born selfish,' Aunt Eunice said, which didn't really fit into the conversation but was something she'd always said about Dad. 'Only thought of himself, couldn't care less what happened to anyone else.'

'That's not true, Aunt,' said Ma. 'Dermot did care, in his way, but he never wanted to *own* people. He believed that everyone should be free to do whatever they wanted.' She added unhappily, 'That was the trouble. I couldn't ever bring myself to give him the freedom he wanted. To my mind, it didn't add up to a proper marriage.'

'Some people are like that with dogs,' Uncle Pat agreed. 'Scared to let them off the lead in case they never come back. Then one day they slip their collars and it's goodbye Bonzo.'

Ma looked close to tears. I glared at Uncle Pat.

Aunt Eunice piped up, 'I don't like dogs. They mess on the pavements and spread diseases. They should be put down.'

'I agree,' said Zak. 'Dogs and silly old women. No use to anyone. They should all be exterminated.'

114

She stared at him in horror. He leered evilly back.

'That's enough!' Gabriel's eyes shot deadly missiles at Zak.

'Oh, I beg your pardon!' Zak clasped his hands together and bowed his head. 'Please forgive me, O gracious Lord.'

He was sending Gabriel up rotten. I held my breath, waiting for the explosion.

It didn't come. Gabriel closed his eyes briefly, in pained distaste, but only said, 'We're getting off the point. All I'm trying to say is that we should keep our main objective right up front, not let ourselves be distracted by the demands of day-to-day living. Don't you agree, Francesca?'

She murmured a reluctant yes, but still looked unhappy.

'With that in mind,' he continued, 'I suggest we enter a short period of purification...'

'Saints preserve us!' exclaimed Uncle Pat under his breath.

'...in order to prepare ourselves for the coming event.'

There was an expectant silence. Zak smiled, half-closing his eyes, and beside him Boris did exactly the same. They looked like a pair of feline zombies.

Jedda yawned.

'What coming event would this be?' Uncle Pat inquired, sweet as treacle pudding.

'All in good time, Patrick. First you have to convince me that you're a worthy receptacle.'

'Receptacle, is it?' Uncle Pat chuckled. 'I've been one of them for years, old son.'

'The operative word is "worthy", Patrick. For that you'll have to stay off the whisky for at least forty-eight hours.'

'Forty-eight hours! Saints, that's a lifetime.'

'Nonetheless it's the task you have to perform in order to qualify.' Gabriel became suddenly decisive. 'Each of you will have a task, according to your special needs. Francesca, yours will be to ignore Christmas.'

'Ignore it? But—'

'No buts. Eunice, yours...' He leaned forward to whisper in her ear. Her eyes widened fearfully. Then she nodded.

'Rose...' He bestowed on me a smile that still made me tingle, despite my doubts. 'Your task will be to help me in what lies ahead.'

'What about Zak and Jedda?' asked Ma.

'They can help Aisling in the kitchen. It's time they learned a little humility.'

Zak uttered a word I'd never heard before but I felt pretty sure it wasn't Venusian. Jedda stared at Gabriel with obvious dismay.

'There won't be all that much to do in the kitchen if we're not having Christmas.' Ma's tone was now definitely tart.

'Bravo!' said Uncle Pat, miming applause.

For one brief second Gabriel showed annoyance. The next he said calmly, 'The meeting's over.

Remember your tasks. Now you must all go and leave me alone with Rose.'

This took them by surprise – though not half so much as it did me – but after a moment they got to their feet and started drifting away. I still found it fairly amazing that everyone did whatever Gabriel told them to do. It was partly instinct, I think. Like a pack of dogs, they recognized him as their natural leader even though they might grumble a bit and make a show of rebelling, like Uncle Pat. But increasingly fear had begun to play a part in it too. They obeyed him because they were afraid of the consequences – whatever they were – if they didn't.

When we were alone I said, 'Will they do them, do you think – the tasks you've set?'

He shrugged. 'If they don't qualify that's their loss, not ours.'

I had to ask. 'This event – does it have some connection with that place we went to on the Common?'

'Come here, Rose.' I shuffled closer. He took my hands. 'Do you believe we can do it?'

He was asking *me*! I said, 'If you mean what I think you mean, I honestly don't know.'

'But are you prepared to try?'

'If that's what you want.'

His eyes blazed. He gripped my fingers. When he spoke again his voice shook with emotion. 'Power, Rose – that's what this is all about. We can do anything, you and I, if we put our minds to it.'

I was transfixed by his expression, but part of me was thinking, *He believes this. It isn't an act. He genuinely believes everything he says.*

I wished now I'd never given him Dad's manuscript to read.

14

Ours was practically the only house in Oakfield Avenue without a lighted Christmas tree in the window. Ma had taken down the one we had and told Uncle Pat to plant it in the back garden. She'd also put the decorations back in the box and removed every single paper chain and sprig of holly, as well as the mistletoe from the hall.

The most amazing thing of all, though, was that Uncle Pat had been on the wagon now for thirty-nine-and-a-half hours. 'I'm doing it for your mother's sake,' he said when I congratulated him. 'Seems to me she's going to need somebody sober around when the balloon goes up.'

'What balloon?'

'She's cracking, Rosie, haven't you noticed? Ever since those two weirdos appeared on the scene. Any minute now the worm will turn.'

'She'd love that,' I said caustically. 'Being called a worm.'

'A figure of speech, that's all. You know I hold

Francesca in high esteem. She's a spanking fine woman.' His eyes became moist with emotion. 'I told Dermot so on many an occasion.'

'Come off it, Uncle Pat, you led him astray.'

'Never! Dermot didn't need leading, he was astray from the day he was born.' He shook his head regretfully. 'He wasn't the man for your mother, Rosie, that was the sadness of it. Dermot's a hawk, Francesca's a homing pigeon. Put a hawk in the pigeon-loft and there's bound to be trouble.'

'Uncle Pat,' I said, 'you wouldn't by any chance be falling for Ma, would you?'

He pinkened slightly. 'Now there's a fancy notion. I wonder what put it into your head?'

'Only that it seems to me you're showing serious signs of devotion, what with giving up whisky for her sake and staying around to protect her interests. And she's definitely more partial towards you than she used to be.'

'Put it this way, Rosie. Your ma needs someone to complicate her life. In the absence of Dermot she'll likely be glad of a substitute, preferably a body that's not too perfect already so that she has something to work on. Seems to me I could fit that bill.'

'And would that suit you too?'

'It might. Fact is, I've reached the age where I'd find it restful to get me feet under a table, preferably in a pair of carpet slippers.'

'Even if they're still warm from somebody else's feet?'

'Sure – provided that somebody else doesn't still want them. Anyway, I reckon I'm more of a warm slipper man than Dermot ever was.'

I tried to see Uncle Pat in a different light, as a surrogate father, but it wasn't easy. I said doubtfully, 'It doesn't sound very romantic.'

'Ah, well. If it's romance you're looking for, you'll have a long wait.' He grimaced, airing his tongue. 'Saints, what I wouldn't give for a drop of the hard stuff! I swear it would sharpen me wits.'

'Don't risk it,' I advised. 'Otherwise you'll be disqualified.'

'Only if Boyo finds out.'

'He'd smell it on your breath.'

Uncle Pat groaned. 'I hope Francesca appreciates the wondrous nature of me sacrifice.'

Another strange sight was Jedda at the kitchen sink, peeling potatoes. Her appearance had changed in the last two days. For a start she wasn't wearing her usual chalky make-up so you could see how many zits she had on her pointed chin. She still wore her black leather jumpsuit, though. If she's human, I thought, she'll soon begin to smell.

She flourished a saucepan full of peeled spuds in front of Aisling. 'These okay?'

'They'll do,' Aisling said grudgingly.

'Anything else?'

'No, thanks. You can go now.'

'Cheers.'

When she had left the kitchen I remarked, 'She looks almost normal today apart from her hair.'

'It's a wig.' Aisling was cutting circles out of pastry and putting them into a tart tin. 'They're both wearing wigs, hadn't you realized? Shift your carcase, Rose, I want to get to the cupboard.'

I moved aside. She took down a jar of mincemeat from the shelf and prised off the lid with a pair of scissors.

I said, 'I did ask Gabriel to make them go, but he said they weren't important.'

'Not to him, no. Not any more. He has other fish to fry.'

I gave her a sharp look. 'Has he told you, then?'

'Told me what?'

'About the landing on...' Suddenly I realized what she was doing and everything else went out of my head. 'Aisling, you're making mince pies!'

'So what?' She went on grimly spooning mincemeat into the pastry cases.

'Gabriel will be furious. You know what he said. We're supposed to be ignoring Christmas.'

She shrugged. 'There's no law says you can only eat mince pies at Christmas.'

I stared at her helplessly. This was open defiance, no doubt about it. She was deliberately flouting Gabriel's orders.

'It'll upset Ma,' I reasoned.

'I don't think so. If I did I wouldn't –'

At this point the doorbell rang. I raced to answer it

before Zak or Jedda could get there in case it was one of the neighbours.

It was Victoria.

'Hi, Rose,' she said, with a bright, expectant smile.

'Did you want something?' I asked ungraciously.

'Only to see you.' She was across the threshold before I had a chance to say it wasn't convenient just now. 'Is there somewhere we can talk?'

I opened the door of the front room, then realized too late it was already occupied by Ma and Gabriel who were seated on the floor, practising deep meditation. Ma looked up immediately when we entered, Gabriel was too far gone to notice.

'Oops, sorry.'

I turned at once and bumped into Victoria, who stood with her mouth open, staring at Gabriel. Just lately he had started dressing like Lawrence of Arabia, in flowing white robes but without the headgear. Heaven knows where he got hold of the outfit, because it certainly didn't belong to Dad. He was also letting his beard grow, and possibly his hair, only it was too early yet to be able to tell. The general effect was decidedly biblical.

I pushed Victoria, who still had her mouth open, out of the room. 'Let's go upstairs.'

When we reached the attic she looked round curiously. By comparison with her bedroom it must have seemed pretty spartan, although Aisling had done her best to brighten up her half with posters and geometric cushions. My bed was plain, apart from the Tigger nightie-case I'd had for years.

'Okay,' I said, somewhat aggressively. 'What did you want to see me about?'

'Gabriel's older than I expected. He must be twenty-five at least.'

'No, he's not,' I snapped, although I had no idea how old Gabriel was. 'He just looks old at the moment because he's growing a beard. Victoria, did you come here to snoop?'

'No!' She looked indignant. 'I came to tell you about Shane.'

'What about Shane?'

She plonked herself down on my bed. 'He took me out for a meal last night. We had chicken cacciatora and tagliatelle and zabaglione. It was an Italian restaurant.'

Trust Victoria to state the obvious. 'So?'

'Aren't you impressed? I bet Matthew's never taken you out for a meal like that.'

'He wouldn't waste his money. Anyway, we don't go out on dates.'

She sat swinging one leg casually back and forth. 'Money doesn't matter to Shane. He's got loads of it, or at least his parents have. You should see their house.'

I stifled a yawn. 'I'm pleased for you, really I am. I hope you'll both be very happy. Now if you wouldn't mind –'

'I must say Gabriel's stupendously good looking. But why does he wear those outlandish clothes?'

I was right, she *had* come to snoop. Telling me about Shane was merely an excuse. 'He likes to dress casually around the house,' I said. 'Besides, they suit his personality.'

'Why was he sitting on the floor with your mother?'

'Ah, well ... they were doing their mental exercises. You know, training the mind.'

'Whatever for?'

While I was still trying to think of an answer there came the most almighty crash. I flung open the door and dashed to the top of the attic stairs. On the landing below Zak was laid out on the floor with Boris peering into his face – and looming over him, arms menacingly akimbo, stood an elderly virago.

'Aunt Eunice!' I flew down the stairs towards them. 'Whatever are you doing?'

'It was my task,' she said triumphantly. 'Gabriel told me to do it.'

As Zak struggled to rise she lashed out with her foot. Taken by surprise, he tripped over Boris, lost his balance and fell down the stairs. There was a series of sickening thuds as his body slammed from wall to bannister and back again, until he reached the final step. Otherwise he made no sound.

'*Bong hai*,' said Aunt Eunice, dusting off her hands.

By now Gabriel and Ma had emerged from the front room. When Zak landed at their feet Ma stared

125

first at him, then up at Aunt Eunice. Zak's red wig, dislodged during his fall, lay halfway down the stairs, looking like the corpse of some mangy animal.

Victoria peered over my shoulder. 'Matthew told me it was weird,' she breathed. 'But I never dreamed it was as weird as this!'

15

Zak had two cracked ribs and a broken arm. Gabriel, still dressed in his Bedouin gear, took him immediately to hospital and Zak came back with his ribs strapped up and his arm in a plaster cast. Without his wig he looked like a convict – he must have shaved his head to make it less hot – and he was obviously scared witless of Aunt Eunice. Every time she entered a room he scuttled out. She, on the other hand, was so pleased with herself that she didn't seem to have noticed she was in disgrace, at least as far as Ma was concerned. Ma said it was lucky Zak was anti the Law, otherwise he might have taken Aunt Eunice to court for GBH. Aunt Eunice said she wished he would. She'd like to see the policeman stupid enough to try to arrest *her*.

I wasn't sure at which point Victoria had slipped out of the house, but it must have been while we were standing in a helpless group around Zak's crumpled body. To be honest I didn't give her a single thought until much later in the day, when Matthew appeared.

'Well, well!' said Aisling when he walked into the kitchen. 'Look who's back, Rose – your devoted swain. It must be wonderful to have such power over men. I envy you, I really do.'

The look he gave her was surprisingly lacking in besottedness. I tried not to show how glad I was to see him. 'What are you doing here, Matthew? We said not until after Christmas.'

'After what?' Aisling asked innocently.

Still ignoring her, he said, 'I met Victoria,' as if that explained everything.

I took him into the front room. This time it was occupied solely by Aunt Eunice, snoozing in an armchair. She opened her eyes to tell Matthew, 'I did it. I carried out my task.'

'Oh, yes?' he said politely. 'What task was that?'

But she had dropped off again. 'Sit down,' I told him.

He sat on the sofa, which had been pushed back against the wall in preparation for tonight's meeting, and looked around. 'I've missed all this,' he said. 'Do you think Gabriel will let me come back?'

The humility in his voice made me suspicious. 'How much did Victoria tell you?' I asked sharply.

'Enough.'

'What do you mean, enough?'

He dropped the humility. 'For me to be sure it's time I came back. You need help, Rose. Besides, I want to know what's going on. For a start, why did Aunt Eunice push that freak down the stairs?'

128

'She didn't exactly push him. He sort of lost his balance when she hit him.'

At the sound of her name Aunt Eunice murmured, '*Bong hai*, it was my task,' without opening her eyes.

Matthew asked, 'Why does she keep on about her task?'

I explained about Gabriel's period of purification, how Ma had been ordered to ignore Christmas and Uncle Pat to stay on the wagon and Aunt Eunice – presumably – to attack Zak.

'What about Aisling?' he asked.

'She doesn't have a task. She left the room before he started handing them out.'

He sighed. 'Rose, there's something you ought to know. I should've told you before, but I was afraid you wouldn't believe me. You remember that night when Gabriel tried to stop me coming here and Aisling stood up for me?'

'I remember.'

'And then Aisling went out for a walk and you said you hadn't realized she had principles?'

'Ye-es.'

'Well, after I left the house I caught them together.'

'Who?'

'Her and Gabriel. They didn't see me, they were too busy quarrelling. Then they went off to that theatre club where Aisling often goes. I know because I followed them.'

I was silent, remembering how when I went into the kitchen that night Gabriel had disappeared...

'I didn't dare go inside in case they spotted me. But a couple of days later, after Gabriel chucked me out of the community, I went back to the club and asked some questions. What I learned was very interesting.'

My mouth was dry, my heart started thumping. 'Go on.'

'For a start, his name isn't Gabriel. It's Jon Walters. And he's an actor. Out of work, only they call it "resting". He and Aisling have been meeting there regularly for about two months.'

'In that case why did they pretend to be strangers?' I demanded.

'Isn't it obvious? Your mother had just started up the community. You'd produced Uncle Pat and he'd been accepted, against all the odds, as a lodger. Ho, ho, thinks Aisling, two can play at that game! So she tells her boyfriend to turn up on the doorstep and act mysterious. That way he's almost certain to be taken for a visitor from Venus.'

It sounded horribly plausible.

He went on, 'Of course I'd guessed all along they must have known each other before. That was obvious from the way they behaved, practically ignoring each other. It wasn't natural. Oh, I know you said he didn't fancy her, but that was wishful thinking. They're both beautiful people, of course they fancied each other.'

Matthew had on his detached, scientific persona. This was a theory he was determined to prove: Beautiful Gabriel + Beautiful Aisling = Meaningful Relationship.

I shook my head. 'Aisling's not that unscrupulous. Whatever her faults, she cares about Ma just as much as I do.'

'But she wouldn't have seen this as any kind of a threat, at least not at the beginning. It would never enter her head he'd take things to these extremes.'

'If he's playing a part,' I said, 'he's playing it amazingly well. All those mind-training exercises...'

'Ah, there's an explanation for that. It seems he's been heavily into that sort of thing for some time. He believes it helps him to learn his lines. What's more, they told me at the theatre club that he always throws himself into every part he plays...'

I said slowly, 'And then I gave him Dad's manuscript...'

'So now he's suffering from even worse delusions than your mother.'

'What about Zak and Jedda? Are they actors too?'

'Hoping to be. So far they haven't been very successful, which is probably why they can't keep up the pretence the way he can. And now Aunt Eunice has kicked one of them downstairs—'

'On Gabriel's orders.'

'Exactly. I'd say their days are numbered.'

Could he be right? I was filled with the most unsettling doubts. But Matthew's face was transparently honest and anyway he regarded all forms of lying as moral cowardice. It would be far more logical to believe him than to believe Gabriel.

Two noises filled the silence, Aunt Eunice's snoring and a strange wailing sound outside the window. It took me a moment to realize what it was.

Carol singers!

> *'We three kings of Orient are;*
> *Bearing gifts we traverse afar...'*

I dived for the front door and flung it open. Ralph and Enid Lehman stood on the step, wearing scarves and overcoats and carrying a lantern. They sang from a shared piece of sheet music:

> *'O-oh, Star of wonder, star of night,*
> *Star with royal beauty bright,*
> *Westward leading –'*

'Oh, shush!' I said fiercely.

'...*Still proceeding –*' Their voices spluttered to a halt. 'Why, what's the matter?'

'I can't explain.' Fearfully I glanced over my shoulder. 'Did you want something?'

'Only to wish you a Happy Christmas.' Enid produced a stack of parcels, gift-wrapped with holly-covered paper and giant green bows. 'We've brought our pressies round.'

'Thanks.' I grabbed them from her and passed

them on to Matthew, who was standing behind me. 'I'm afraid we don't have yours ready yet.'

'It doesn't matter.' Ralph held the lantern towards my face. 'You all right, Rose?'

'Fine.' I started to close the door.

'Happy Christmas, then...'

'Same to you.' I slammed the door shut and put on the chain.

When I turned around Matthew was looking at me with a kindly, almost pitying, expression.

He said, 'You know what my mother told me? That sometimes kids who have a mentally ill parent are so afraid of people finding out they take a self-imposed vow of silence. She says it's a well-known fact. I reckon that's what you and Aisling—'

'Have you been talking to your mother about us? Oh, Matthew, you *promised*!'

He flushed, but said obstinately, 'You're just proving my point, Rose.'

At that moment, luckily for him, Ma came out of the kitchen. 'Was that somebody at the door?' she inquired. 'Oh hello, Matthew. I thought you'd deserted us.'

'The reason I stayed away,' he said, still a little pink, 'is that I was told I wasn't welcome here any more.'

'Rubbish.' Ma's tone was brisk. 'You're welcome any time, Matthew, you know you are. You'll stay for supper?'

'Thanks, Mrs Kelly.'

'It's ready now. I'm just going to tell Aunt Eunice.'

133

When she had disappeared into the front room he muttered, 'She's better, almost like her old self.'

Before I could comment Gabriel came floating down the stairs in his long white robe. I snatched the presents Matthew was holding and hid them behind my back but Gabriel gave no sign that he had spotted them. When he saw Matthew he said calmly, 'Ah, the return of the Prodigal. We must kill the fatted calf. By the way, Rose, you can tell your mother that Zak has left us. He clearly wasn't suited to our way of life.' He floated on into the kitchen.

Matthew murmured, 'What did I tell you? He's finally flipped. Gone right over the edge.'

After supper we assembled in the front room. Jedda was still with us, but she had left off her wig, revealing mouse-coloured hair, lank and split-ended. Despite the leather jumpsuit she looked downright ordinary. I wondered why she had stayed behind now that Zak had gone; but then I saw the way she gazed at Gabriel and realized she was still in thrall to him.

'Tonight,' Gabriel began, 'is Christmas Eve.'

'I thought,' Aisling said crisply, 'we weren't supposed to be celebrating Christmas?'

'We're having our own celebration,' he said. 'Nothing to do with Christmas, except we shall be making use of the existing vibrations.'

'Vibrations?' Matthew repeated. His manner suggested the shrewd investigator rather than the detached observer he used to be, but Gabriel didn't seem to notice.

'At Christmas,' said Gabriel, 'there's always a special charge in the atmosphere, a sense of antici-pation, an extra surge of power. It's important we capitalize on that.'

'Some people,' Uncle Pat said glumly, 'have a good time at Christmas. They enjoy themselves.'

'Gorging themselves sick and drinking each other under the table.' Gabriel's tone was contemptuous. 'Our celebration will take a different form.'

'Pity,' said Uncle Pat.

'Are you going to give us another task?' Aunt Eunice asked hopefully.

'That won't be necessary, Eunice. You've already proved yourself worthy of enlightenment.'

'What kind of enlightenment?' Ma sounded ap-prehensive.

'Patience, Francesca. All will soon become clear to you.'

He was beginning to talk like a character in one of those early Charlton Heston movies. Give him a long curly beard and he'd have been perfect as Moses, commanding the Red Sea to roll back and let through the Israelites. Matthew was right: he'd gone over the edge. It was Gabriel we were playing along with now, not Ma.

I asked nervously, 'When will our celebrations begin?'

'Very shortly, Rose. In fact I see no reason why

they shouldn't begin right now.' He blew out the candle and rose to his feet, which were bare apart from a pair of Jesus sandals. 'Come with me.'

'Are we going on somewhere?' asked Jedda, looking bemused.

'We are going on,' Gabriel said magisterially, 'to Braddon Common.'

16

We dressed in coats, boots and scarves. When we were ready Ma looked at Gabriel's bare feet and said, 'You can't go out like that, you'll catch your death of cold. Where are your shoes?'

He stared at her in surprise. She had never spoken to him in quite that tone of voice before. But he obviously saw the sense in what she said because he went straight upstairs and came back three minutes later wearing his trainers. They looked odd with his flowing robes but nobody laughed. We didn't dare.

Like the Pied Piper he led us through the streets of Braddon. Ma and Jedda came next, then Uncle Pat on his own. I walked with Aunt Eunice, who kept telling me I needn't be afraid because if anyone assaulted me she'd give them a sharp dose of *bong hai*. Behind us came Matthew and Aisling, but they weren't talking.

Because it was Christmas Eve there were plenty of people about, either turning out of the pubs or

137

streaming towards the churches for Midnight Mass, or in some cases both. But we were headed for the Common and heaven knew what pagan rites.

It was a clear night, frosty but windless. Venus hovered above the horizon, brilliant yet mysterious in the dark blue sky. I could not get the tune of that carol out of my head and even found myself humming it under my breath:

> 'Star of wonder, star of night,
> Star with royal beauty bright ...'

'Venus isn't a star,' Matthew pointed out, close on my heels. 'It's a planet.'

'I'm aware of that,' I retorted. 'But "planet of wonder" doesn't scan. You've no sense of poetry, Matthew.'

'So you're always telling me. It's not my fault I have a logical mind.'

I was glad he'd come back. It felt good to be sniping at each other the way we'd always done.

A surprise awaited us on the Common. The light of the moon, almost as bright as day, showed us we were not the only ones to venture there on Christmas Eve. About twenty people were already clustered in the middle of the open space, shivering and chattering amongst themselves. When we arrived they stopped chattering to stare.

Gabriel held up his hand. Obediently we came to a halt. He addressed the other group in impressive, sonorous tones. 'Good evening. I don't know what you're doing here but I'm afraid you'll have to leave. We've come on important business.'

'We was here first.' A bearded man detached himself from the others and confronted Gabriel. 'Anyroad, this is our site, always has been. So push off, prat.'

'How rude!' Aunt Eunice bristled beside me. I got ready to grab her in case she took it into her head to get physical.

'What do you mean, your site?' Gabriel asked coldly.

'We been coming here for years, mate. Since before you was born, most likely.'

His supporters tittered appreciatively. They were all ages, ranging from a wrinkled crone in a tartan cloak to a baby carried papoose-style on its mother's back.

Gabriel's eyes gleamed in the moonlight. 'And may I ask why you come here?'

'Whay we come heah?' The bearded man mimicked Gabriel's actorish accent. 'Yes, I'll tell you why, your Highness. We come to keep watch. Somebody has to do it so's the rest of you can sleep safe in your beds.' He gave a short laugh. 'Ho yes, if it weren't for us you'd be in trouble, believe me!'

The others murmured agreement. They were definitely Rentamob.

Matthew muttered in my ear, 'UFO watchers. Cranks.'

'If they're cranks,' I said, 'what does that make us?'

He didn't answer.

Gabriel said, 'It seems likely that our aims may coincide, in which case you may be interested to join us.'

139

'Join you?' Bearded Man's tone was scornful. 'Why should we want to join you, mate? We're the official party.'

Gabriel smiled, unperturbed. 'Ah, but we have more recent information than you do. If you're serious you can't really afford to exclude us.'

Bearded Man squared his shoulders. Of the two Gabriel was by far the more impressive leader. For a start he stood a good head taller. Also he had an air of confident superiority.

By contrast, Bearded Man seemed all bluster. 'Why, what do you know that we don't?' he demanded.

'Are you acquainted with Venus?'

He looked suspicious. 'Venus who?'

Gabriel gestured to the sky.

'Oh ... yeah. We know all about Venus.'

'But do you know about Dermot Kelly?'

Ma gave a muffled exclamation. She would have stepped forward if Uncle Pat had not restrained her.

Bearded Man glowered at Gabriel. 'You mean the Irishman, the bloke who used to come here with his telescope? Yeah, we know about him. Haven't seen him for a while, though.'

'No, you wouldn't have.' Gabriel was totally in command now. The other group was hanging on to his every word and he knew it. 'Three months ago there was a landing very close to this exact spot, when Dermot Kelly experienced a more than usually close encounter. The precise details of what happened are unknown to us, but we have subsequently learned that he was transported back to Venus.'

They gaped at him. Even Bearded Man was struck dumb.

'No doubt you're wondering how we know this.' Gabriel paused to look round at their faces, clearly revelling in the effect his words were having on them. 'We know because he has recently been in touch with his wife and conveyed to her several important messages. This –' he raised his hand to indicate Ma – 'is Mrs Kelly.'

All eyes swivelled to stare at her. She stared back, her face ghostly white in the moonlight.

'And these are his daughters.' He pointed to Aisling and me. 'They'll testify to the truth of what I'm saying.'

I wanted to shout, 'No, we won't!' but the whole scene seemed somehow portentous and I was reluctant to be the one to break the spell. Aisling too stayed silent, perhaps for the same reason.

'What did they do to him?' A boy about ten years old spoke from deep inside a padded jacket several sizes too large. 'Did they take him prisoner?'

'Shut up, Kev,' Bearded Man growled in a fatherly tone. Nonetheless he relayed the question to Gabriel. 'Did they take him prisoner?'

'Not exactly,' Gabriel replied. 'The messages received by Mrs Kelly indicate he's being trained as an agent so that he may return to assist in the salvation of the human race. The influence of Venus is benign. Its inhabitants mean us no harm.'

141

'We know that,' Bearded Man said gruffly. 'We always come here in a friendly spirit – always have done, haven't we?' He appealed to his supporters, but they were taking little notice of him now. Their eyes were fixed on Gabriel.

The wrinkled crone spoke up in a cracked, strident voice. 'Is that why you came here tonight, because you're expecting him back?'

Gabriel shrugged. 'Shall we say the signs are propitious?'

Everyone looked up at the sky. The only craft in sight was a passenger jet flying high above us, lights flashing, on its way to Heathrow. Aunt Eunice tugged at my sleeve. 'Did he say Dermot's coming back tonight?'

'Sssh, Aunt.'

'But we don't want him here. He'll spoil everything. I keep telling Francesca she's better off without him.'

A girl wearing a knitted hat pulled low over her forehead asked nervously, 'Will they be wanting more of us to go and train as agents? Only it wouldn't be too convenient for me just now. I'm starting a new job after Christmas.'

'Don't worry, Lorraine,' said Bearded Man. 'They'll be looking for a certain sort of person, I expect, with special qualities. Isn't that right?' He was deferring to Gabriel now.

'There's no way of knowing who will be chosen. No doubt they have their own method of selection.' Gabriel took up a stance with hands folded across his

chest and eyes turned upwards. 'I suggest we prepare ourselves for tonight's vigil.'

As if by instinct everyone fanned out to form a
circle around his priest-like figure. Matthew, Aisling,
Aunt Eunice and I found ourselves separated from
Ma and Uncle Pat, who were directly opposite. When I
looked across at Ma's bleak face I began to feel angry.

I hissed at Aisling, 'I hope you're satisfied?'

'I don't know what you mean,' she said.

'Oh yes, you do!'

From the other side Matthew muttered, 'The
game's up, Aisling. We know it was you who invited
Gabriel into the community...'

'We know he's an actor...'

'We even know his real name.'

'How could you do it, Aisling?'

'Because I felt sorry for him.' Her face crumpled.
'And before, when I'd told him about Ma, he seemed
so sympathetic. I thought he'd be an ally. He
promised to help me. I wasn't to know he'd carry
things too far.'

'The guy's unhinged,' Matthew said sternly. 'Surely
you must have realized the way he acted wasn't
normal?'

'How could I? I'm not even sure what *is* normal any
more. First Dad starts acting strangely, then Ma—'
She choked on a sob.

I squeezed her arm. 'It's my fault as much as yours.
I was the one who gave him Dad's manuscript to read.'

'What we have to decide,' Matthew said, 'is how

we're going to – ' He broke off as Gabriel turned to stare in our direction. Although we were talking quietly our voices must have carried. Aisling caught her breath.

After one long, malevolent look he turned his attention back to the heavens. Everyone else followed suit, including me, although I hadn't a clue what we were supposed to be looking for. Some kind of a UFO, I supposed. But as another jet crossed the sky I couldn't help thinking that Braddon Common would be a rotten choice for a landing anyway. Surely no Venusian in his right mind would choose such a busy flight-path . . .

'*Oh, this is ridiculous!*'

For a moment I thought I must have spoken the words myself. But then I realised it was Ma's voice that had said them.

She stepped forward to confront Gabriel, hands on her hips, her square chin stuck out. 'I never heard such rubbish.' She raised her voice to address the rest of the circle. 'Dermot Kelly hasn't gone to Venus. He walked out on me, that's all. Walked out on a stale marriage to a woman he didn't love and went to live his own life somewhere else. It's taken me a long time to accept the fact, but now I have and I can't be doing with all this Venus nonsense. It isn't my way of thinking, it never was, and it's no use me pretending any longer. I've had enough.'

There was a stunned silence. Then Uncle Pat gave

a cheer. 'That's my girl! Give it to 'em straight, Francesca.'

She turned back to Gabriel. 'As for you, you should be ashamed of yourself, taking advantage of people who don't know any better. It's high time you went back where you came from – and I don't mean Venus!'

'Oh, great!' crowed Matthew. 'A complete recovery – and she's done it all by herself.'

Gabriel stared at Ma as if she had turned into Frankenstein's monster. 'You're not well, Francesca . . .'

'Yes, I am! Never felt better.' She looked scornfully round the circle. 'Nothing's going to happen here tonight, you can take my word for it. This young man –' she pointed at Gabriel – 'will take you all for a proper ride, given half a chance. Oh, we've got the earth in a right old mess, I grant you that, but it's no use waiting around for aliens to come zooming down from outer space and put things right. We have to do the job ourselves – and that's the *real* message from Venus, the only message you're likely to get.' She glared at everyone, breathing hard.

An excited babble broke out. Uncle Pat slapped Ma on the back, grinning all over his face. 'What's happening?' Aunt Eunice demanded. 'What's she saying? Why is she so cross with Gabriel?'

'Because she's come to her senses at last.' I felt as if I had drunk about a quart of champagne and it was fizzing away inside me. 'She's back to being Ma again.'

She called to us above the hubbub. 'I don't know

about the rest of you, but I'm cold and I'm tired and I want to go home. And when I get there the first thing I'm going to do is put up the decorations again and get that turkey out of the deep freeze. It won't be thawed out in time for tomorrow, but we'll have our Christmas a day late if needs be. Patrick, you can dig up that tree.'

'With pleasure, Fran darlin'.' He flung his arms round her in an ecstatic hug.

I raced to join them, and after a moment's hesitation Aisling did the same. The four of us swung round and round, then broke up briefly to gather a bemused Aunt Eunice into the circle while Matthew stood by, looking embarrassed.

All talking at once we started to move away from the site. It was not until we reached the edge of the clearing that I glanced back over my shoulder. Rentamob had stopped watching us and were whispering among themselves. Gabriel stood apart, a striking figure in his long white robe, his head thrown back defiantly. He looked very impressive, quite otherworldly. Suddenly I felt my doubts returning...

But then Matthew grabbed my hand and pulled me away. We ran until we caught up with the others.

17

'We've no need to disband the community entirely,'
Ma said on Christmas morning – *our* Christmas
morning, a day later than the rest of the world's.
'Aunt Eunice says she'd like to stay and I've told
her that's all right with me as long as she gives up
violence. We can't live in fear of being thrown
downstairs every time one of us disagrees with
her.'

Aunt Eunice, in quilted dressing gown and curlers,
looked a little smug. 'It was only self-defence,' she
murmured.

'So you keep telling us,' Ma said shortly. 'But it
looked remarkably like aggression to me. So any
more *bong hai* and out you go, Aunt. Understood?'

Aunt Eunice nodded and sighed. Despite everything, it seemed to me that Gabriel had had a few
good ideas, and making Aunt Eunice less fearful was
one of them.

'What about me?' Jedda inquired. Her nose and
eyes were still red from the crying jag she'd been on

147

since she left Gabriel on Braddon Common in the early hours of yesterday morning. Apparently he had ordered her to go and said he would follow later, but he never did.

Ma regarded her doubtfully. 'Surely you've a home of your own to go to?'

Jedda shook her head. She looked like a pathetic waif. How could I ever have managed to delude myself she could be a visitor from outer space?

'Where do your parents live?' Ma asked.

'My mum lives in Manchester, but I can't go there. She's got married again and I don't get on with my stepfather.' She sniffed loudly, wiping her nose on her leather sleeve.

Aisling got up, collected the box of paper tissues that sat permanently on the dresser, and silently handed it to Jedda. She was not nearly so unfriendly towards her now that Gabriel had gone.

'Don't you have any other family?' Ma inquired. 'Relations you *do* get on with?'

Jedda sniffed again. 'I've got a Gran and Grandad in Essex. They're my Dad's people. I get on with them okay, but it's pretty dull where they live, hardly any nightlife at all.'

I could see Ma's mind ticking over and knew exactly what she was thinking. This was because she had gone back to being her old predictable self again, and the look she gave Jedda was exactly the same look she used to give Dad when he was being particularly feckless.

'The problem is, Jedda,' she said, 'we only have four bedrooms, counting the attic. That means we –'

Aunt Eunice interrupted. 'I'm not having her in my room. I'm too old to share. It's not right at my time of life...'

'She's not sharing with anyone,' Ma said firmly. Today she'll telephone her grandparents to say she's going to visit them. Everyone should be with their own family at Christmas.'

'But –' Jedda began.

'Good, that's settled. But first you can help me clear the table. We've a lot to do this morning.'

Ma was full of purpose again. She behaved as if the whole bizarre episode had never taken place, but according to Matthew it wasn't so much that she had suppressed it as put it behind her. He said he now thought Aisling and I had been right to let her come back to her senses in her own good time. He even thought Gabriel might have helped without meaning to. As for me, I couldn't be bothered to analyse what had happened. I was just thankful it was all over.

I called Victoria. She was on my conscience again and I wanted to put things right between us. When she answered I said, 'Hi, it's Rose. I just wanted to wish you a late Happy Christmas.'

'Same to you. How did it go?' She lowered her voice. 'Was it gruesome?'

'No, it was fine.' I didn't bother to tell her we hadn't even started yet. 'How's Shane?'

'Great. We're going out to a club tomorrow night. Why don't you come with us and bring Gabriel?'

'Actually, he's gone.'

'Gone where?'

'No idea.'

'You poor thing! You must be devastated.'

'Not really.' I tried to sound bored and world-weary. 'I've decided to give up older men. In future I shall stick to Matthew.'

'Dear old Matthew. Still, he's not exactly quiver-making, is he? I mean, you've known each other for years without anything happening.'

I said enigmatically, 'Oh, Matthew has hidden depths. You'd be surprised.' Before she had time to query this I added, 'Can't stop now, I have to go out. See you, Vic.' I replaced the receiver and grabbed my jacket and scarf.

On my way down the front path I bumped into Uncle Pat, who had just popped next door to invite the Lehmans in for a drink. 'Going somewhere, Rosie?' he asked.

'I have to fetch Matthew. Ma wants him to come to our Christmas dinner. I know he already had one yesterday, with his mother, but that was at an old folks' home where she was helping out, so today will be more of a family affair.'

'A family affair,' Uncle Pat repeated, his eyes growing suspiciously moist. 'Ah, the sweetest words in the English language – and also the saddest, to a lonely old outsider like meself.'

I knew he was deliberately tugging at my heart-strings. Nonetheless I felt an overwhelming rush of affection for him. 'I'm glad I asked you to come here, Uncle Pat. It's the best thing I ever did. Anyway, you're only an outsider because you've spent your life sailing round the world. Now's your chance to settle down.'

He gave me an anxious look. 'You don't think I'm trying to take your father's place?'

'Of course not. Listen, if you and Ma want to get married that's okay by me.'

'Trouble is, Rosie, we still don't know where Dermot is. That means your mother won't be free to marry again for at least a couple of years.'

'It's a long time to wait,' I agreed.

He grinned sheepishly. 'Who said anything about waiting?'

I gave him a hug. Okay, so he wasn't perfect, but I had a gut feeling that Ma would be a lot happier with Uncle Pat than she ever was with Dad. Anyway, as he had said himself, she wouldn't want anyone *too* perfect.

It was good celebrating Christmas a day later than everyone else. The people I passed in the street looked jaded and bad-tempered, stuffed to the eyeballs with rich food and too much television. I found Matthew slumped in a chair, watching kids' programmes. His mother was out on a job so he was more than ready to come round to our house.

151

As we walked home he asked, 'Did you hear the news?'

'What news?'

'UFO sighted hovering over Braddon Common on Christmas Eve. According to some reports it actually landed. Of course it's mass delusion – and *we* know how the rumour started, don't we?'

'I suppose so,' I said doubtfully. 'Matthew, I think it might be best if you didn't mention this at home.'

'Why not? Your mother's fully recovered now. It can't do her any harm.'

'All the same, I'd rather you didn't. I don't want anything to spoil today. I want it to be the best Christmas we've ever had.'

Matthew looked surprised. 'Even though your father isn't home?'

'I've accepted that. To be honest, it doesn't worry me any more – at least, not so much as it did. As long as Ma's back to normal I can cope with Dad being missing.'

He whistled through his teeth. 'It never ceases to amaze me, the toughness of the human spirit.'

'God, but you're pompous!' I said affectionately.

My wish was granted: it was the best Christmas we'd ever had. As I looked round the table at Uncle Pat carving the turkey, Aunt Eunice knocking back the Liebfraumilch and Matthew slipping bits of ham to Boris under the table, I reflected how strange it was that good things sometimes come out of bad. I wouldn't have wanted to be without the community now, provided it stayed more or less the way it was, and I didn't think Ma would either. She presided over the table with a watchful eye, as much in charge as she'd ever been, and wore the silly paper hat on her head like a crown.

Nobody mentioned Gabriel, but I couldn't help wondering if the UFO that was supposed to have landed on the Common had transported him back to Venus? It would explain why he never came back to collect the expensive-looking tape recorder we found in the wardrobe. And he was definitely psyched up to go, no doubt about that. I only hoped it lived up to his expectations.

There's a postscript to this story. About two months later Ma announced at breakfast, 'I've had a letter from your father.'

Aisling gaped at her, I nearly dropped my tea cup. Uncle Pat said hopefully, 'From Dermot? Does he say where we can contact him?'

'A P.O. box number in Venice.' Ma waved an airmail envelope. She didn't look at all upset. 'Not the Italian Venice. A place called Venice Beach, in California.'

'America?' I said incredulously. 'What's he doing there?'

'I'm not sure. But he says the climate suits him and the people are more receptive to new ideas than they are over here. He sends his love to you two girls and hopes we can all go out to visit him sometime.'

'I shan't go,' declared Aunt Eunice. 'They have gangsters in America.'

She had more or less reverted to her old self again now, except she seemed happier than she used to be. I wasn't sure about Boris. Sometimes his yellow eyes had a strangely distant look.

'Does Dad say he's sorry?' Aisling demanded.

'Not in so many words. But then you know your father.' Ma placed the letter in the middle of the table. 'You can read it if you like. There's nothing private.'

I didn't want to read it. My feelings about Dad were still too confused. I wasn't sure if I hated him for what he did to Ma or if I thought he was right to go away. I was afraid that if I read the letter I might get angry again.

Suddenly I saw him quite clearly in my mind's eye. He was sitting on a beach in the moonlight, dressed in a pair of frayed khaki shorts, observing a whole new skyful of stars. He looked happy. He looked as if he belonged there.

And it was Venice, not Venus . . .

Okay, so it must be a coincidence the names were so similar.

Unless we had a wineglass that couldn't spell?